Here's what critics a[re saying about] Leslie Langtry

"I laughed so hard I cried on multiple occasions while reading MARSHMALLOW S'MORE MURDER! Girl Scouts, the CIA, and the Yakuza... what could possibly go wrong?"
—Fresh Fiction

"Darkly funny and wildly over the top, this mystery answers the burning question, 'Do assassin skills and Girl Scout merit badges mix...' one truly original and wacky novel!"
—RT BOOK REVIEWS

"Those who like dark humor will enjoy a look into the deadliest female assassin and PTA mom's life."
—Parkersburg News

"Mixing a deadly sense of humor and plenty of sexy sizzle, Leslie Langtry creates a brilliantly original, laughter-rich mix of contemporary romance and suspense in *'Scuse Me While I Kill This Guy.*"
—Chicago Tribune

"The beleaguered soccer mom assassin concept is a winner, and Langtry gets the fun started from page one with a myriad of clever details."
—Publisher's Weekly

BOOKS BY LESLIE LANGTRY

Merry Wrath Mysteries:
Merit Badge Murder
Mint Cookie Murder
Scout Camp Murder (short story in the Killer Beach Reads collection)
Marshmallow S'More Murder
Movie Night Murder
Mud Run Murder

Greatest Hits Mysteries:
'Scuse Me While I Kill This Guy
Guns Will Keep Us Together
Stand By Your Hitman
I Shot You Babe
Paradise By The Rifle Sights
Snuff the Magic Dragon
My Heroes Have Always Been Hitmen
Have Yourself a Deadly Little Christmas (a holiday short story)

Aloha Lagoon Mysteries:
Ukulele Murder
Ukulele Deadly

Other Works:
Sex, Lies, & Family Vacations

Hanging Tree Tales YA horror novels:
Hell House
Tyler's Fate
Witch Hill
The Teacher

MUD RUN MURDER

A Merry Wrath Mystery

USA TODAY BESTSELLING AUTHOR
Leslie Langtry

MUD RUN MURDER
Copyright © 2017 by Leslie Langtry
Cover design by Janet Holmes

Published by Gemma Halliday Publishing
All Rights Reserved. Except for use in any review, the reproduction or utilization of this work in whole or in part in any form by any electronic, mechanical, or other means, now known or hereafter invented, including xerography, photocopying and recording, or in any information storage and retrieval system is forbidden without the written permission of the publisher, Gemma Halliday.

This is a work of fiction. Names, characters, places, and incidents are either the product of the author's imagination or are used fictitiously, and any resemblance to actual persons, living or dead, business establishments, or events or locales is entirely coincidental.

This book is dedicated to the amazing staff and volunteers of the Girl Scouts of Eastern Iowa & Western Illinois who have given me some rich and rewarding (and often hilarious) memories. I feel incredibly lucky to have been a young Girl Scout, Troop Leader and Volunteer with this group over the decades. And a special shout out to Mahlon Sibert—the BEST EVER Ranger at Camp Conestoga/Camp Liberty—who is retiring this year. The place won't be quite the same without him.

CHAPTER ONE

If you ever are given a choice between defending yourself against two hit men in a back alley in Qatar, armed only with a wire coat hanger (don't ask), and giving a pill to a cat, I'd suggest you go with the former. And I'm speaking from experience. In both situations.

Philby, my Hitler-doppelganger cat, could keep her mouth closed as tightly as two steel rods fused together and doused with water in Antarctica. It turned out that she didn't like pills. Unfortunately for her, the slipped disc in her back wouldn't stop shooting pain up her spine until she took them.

Maybe I should have tried Kevlar oven mitts? The cat hadn't bitten me yet, but she was struggling like a pissed-off feline on speed.

"I'm doing this for your own good," I insisted through gritted teeth.

The vet had suggested (while suppressing hysterical laughter) wrapping her tightly in a towel with only her face exposed. I'd done that, but all I got was an angry cat burrito whose lips refused to budge. I tried to figure out a way to hold the beast *and* pry her lips open. Once you got past the lips, there was a whole new litany of problems, including having to deal with the tiny, interlocking teeth, inserting the pill, and getting her to swallow the damn thing. This venture made the planning of D-day look like a walk in the park. A literal walk in the park.

"Philby! You won't get better if you don't take this! The vet said this stuff will relax your muscles, allowing the disc to slip back into place!"

Have you ever tried reasoning with a cat? In my career in the CIA, I'd had to reason with a Belgian nudist wielding a meat cleaver, a paranoid Mexican drug lord who'd had way too much LSD and believed he was a sloth, and a very hostile nun in Chile brandishing knitting needles. None of them were this stubborn. Well, that's not entirely true. The nun was behaving like a toddler throwing a tantrum. But that wasn't the point.

I tucked Philby, still wrapped in a towel, under my left arm. Bracing against the counter for the illusion of some semblance of support, I held the upper jaw in my left hand and the lower jaw in my right and squeezed. The lips parted with a juicy *smack*, but the teeth wouldn't give.

An idea popped into my head. While still struggling with the cat in the towel, I said the one word that would open her mouth. A name that usually sent her into a vicious hissing spree and, most of the time, ended with her on her side, helpless and spent.

"Bobb," I said directly to her. I even went the extra mile and pronounced the second *b*. She didn't like the name because a guy named Bobb once tried to kill her. I couldn't blame the cat.

Philby hissed, and I wedged my fingers between her teeth. Using my left index finger, I shoved the pill into her mouth and then slammed it shut and held it closed.

"What are you doing?" Rex appeared behind me. He must've used his key to get in.

"Great timing," I said as my cat squirmed, hissing in my arms. "A few moments earlier, and you could've helped."

"Why is Philby foaming at the mouth?" he asked.

Philby *was* foaming at the mouth. Really foaming. She looked like a rabid feline dictator who'd just swallowed saliva-activated bubble bath.

"Oh crap," I said as I leaned forward and blew into her face.

The cat's eyes grew wide, but she swallowed. I don't know why that worked. The vet had suggested it. I can tell you that if anyone held my face shut and blew on it, swallowing wouldn't be the first thing to pop into my head.

"It's tramadol," I explained as I unwrapped my furious cat. "If she holds it in her mouth and doesn't swallow it foams up." I ran the towel over her mouth. "Which is kind of a bizarre side effect, if you ask me."

Philby gave me a death stare that in her mind probably paralyzed me with fear, but in reality made me wonder what Rex was doing over here. The hunky detective (who was also my boyfriend) lived directly across the street from me.

"Why are you here?" I tossed the towel on the counter and scooped up Martini—Philby's kitten who looked a lot like Elvis. *She* still loved me. Hmm...I'd have to sleep with one eye open tonight. Philby was probably plotting something.

"We have a date." Rex kissed me on the forehead.

"Oh wow! I totally forgot." And I had, but I was going to blame my evil, non-pill-swallowing cat for that.

"Pizza's on its way," Rex said over his shoulder as he headed for the door.

"I'll be there in a few!" I shouted, but the door had already closed behind him.

Why had I forgotten about our date? It was Friday, and on Friday nights we always had pizza and rented a movie. Sometimes I took the cats, and my awesome boyfriend even had a litter box and food for them.

Martini suddenly decided I was evil. She hissed at me as she jumped down to the floor and, with her head held high, trotted off down the hallway to find her injured mother. So I was guessing the felines wouldn't be joining us tonight.

It took me about fifteen minutes to take a quick shower and get dressed. I slipped out the door and crossed the street. The pizza guy must've arrived because a run-down pickup truck sat in Rex's driveway. Just as I passed the car, I saw it.

The pizza delivery dude was slumped over the steering wheel, and it looked like there was a small-caliber gunshot wound to the temple. Glassy eyes stared at his lap. He couldn't have survived a gunshot at that close a range, but I reached in to take his pulse to be sure. Yup. Dead. I dropped to a crouch behind the truck, in case whoever had murdered this kid was still around.

I hadn't heard a gunshot. But then, I had been in the shower. Did Rex know?

And that's when it hit me.

The dead guy wasn't in *my* driveway. For the first time in a while, I had nothing to do with a murder! Woo-hoo!

It was wrong of me to do the end zone dance and even worse of me to high-five myself (which, if you haven't tried, isn't easy to do). But I couldn't help it. This was just too good to be true. Well, maybe not for the pizza guy, but definitely for me.

For the first time, Rex would be the one scrutinized. Not me! Yay!

Not that I was really worried about that. Rex was a detective with the Who's There, Iowa police department. Suspicion wouldn't really fall on me like it would if the pizza guy had just parked about fifty feet in the opposite direction.

I stopped dancing (mainly because it made me look like an idiot) and headed for Rex's front door. Yes, I was evil. I could *not* wait to tell him what had just happened. Rub it in his face a little.

I stepped onto his stoop and reached for the doorknob. But it wasn't there.

I mean, of course it was there. It was just forward a little farther because the door was open. That seemed bad because maybe whoever shot the delivery kid was in Rex's house, getting ready to shoot him.

I slipped inside the doorway and pressed myself up against the wall. It was very quiet. That, in my experience as a spy, wasn't good. At all. Rex was in trouble, and if I hadn't been grandstanding over the dead guy in the driveway, I could've saved him.

Footsteps echoed in the hallway, and I dropped into a crouch, placing my hands on either side of my feet. As the footsteps grew close enough, my left leg shot out and tripped the intruder.

His body went down with a thud, but not before he pulled a gun and pointed it at me.

"Hold on." Rex looked up at me from the flat of his back as he hit the mute button on his phone and lowered the gun. "What the hell are you doing?"

"Sorry! Are you okay?"

"I think I would've been safer if you had been the intruder."

I took that as a compliment. I helped him to his feet with some vaguely muttered apologies, and he went back to his call.

"Young man in his late teens," he said. "Send a forensic squad and call Dr. Body."

He ended the call and looked at me with an arched eyebrow.

"I thought the killer was coming for you," I mumbled.

"I can see that." He brushed off his shorts and T-shirt. "Thank God I have you to protect me."

"I see that you have a dead body in your driveway," I said. "Did you notice that it's not in *my* driveway for once?"

Rex nodded. "How could I miss it?"

"I know it's wrong..." I said. "But yay, me, right?" I held my hand up for a high five.

I didn't get one.

"Merry." My boyfriend sighed. "I'm sure you're excited that for once dead bodies aren't popping up all around you..."

I frowned. "Well, I'd hardly say *all* around me. It's not my fault that—"

Rex interrupted. "But now I have a crime scene, an investigation to begin, and family members to notify."

He looked at me for a moment before I agreed. I knew he was right. Damn.

Two squad cars and a small Prius pulled up. Dr. Soo Jin Body, the drop-dead gorgeous lady coroner, got out and, upon seeing me, smiled. If I had hackles...whatever those were...they'd be up. Which was probably unfair since Soo Jin was always so nice to me. To everybody. But that was the problem, because she was also too nice to two men in particular—Rex and my CIA handler, Riley. Make that my *former* CIA handler.

"Bond and Moneypenny are doing great, Merry!"

Considering that her two kittens were once my two kittens, and furthermore, prodigy of the aforementioned evil Hitler cat, I tried to be nice. But I hadn't given them away to the striking woman. Riley had. I'd like to think she'd hypnotized him.

"I'm glad." I faked a smile.

Two officers I didn't know got out of one of the squad cars. Kevin Dooley exited the other one. Kevin had been in my grade in high school. He was an idiot then and...well...was still an idiot now. He tossed a bag of chips into the squad car and wiped his hands on his uniform before joining Dr. Soo Jin and the rest of us. As usual, he breathed through his mouth. A caveman had more personality.

"Any idea when this happened?" Soo Jin asked as she reached in and touched the dead man's throat.

"I already did that," I offered, but everyone ignored me.

"I left Merry's house twenty minutes ago. The truck wasn't here then," Rex explained. "I saw him pull in and went into the kitchen to grab my wallet. When I came out here, he was dead."

"It looks like a very small caliber," she said. "I'd guess a .22. The bullet entered here." The coroner pointed at the temple. "But I don't see an exit wound."

We all leaned in to see. Kevin put his hands on the car door, and I drove an elbow into his side. Mostly because he shouldn't touch the car without gloves, and also because he had once been my lab partner in biology and he'd eaten part of the starfish we were dissecting—resulting in a D grade. For both of us.

"Fingerprints," I hissed.

He frowned in confusion. "You want me to dust for fingerprints?" His voice was flat like his brain.

"Officer Dooley," Rex chastised. "Your fingerprints are contaminating the crime scene. Please don't touch anything."

Kevin slowly removed his hands. I was pretty sure that was the processing speed for him. One of the other officers began to dust the vehicle around the driver's side of the car.

It was great to watch Rex work, considering every time I'd witnessed it in the past, it was because the corpse was attached to me. Well, not attached, but on my doorstep, in my driveway, flung across the hood of my car while I was driving…that sort of thing.

He was a very thorough detective and missed nothing—and was super hot in his black, slightly fitted T-shirt, and his dark hair and blue eyes. He walked around the truck, pointing out stuff to the three policemen.

Automatically the wheels in my head started to turn. Who'd want to kill this pizza delivery guy? This was a small town in the middle of Iowa. We didn't have drive-by shootings here. In fact we had very little crime here at all until I showed up.

But this time, this guy wasn't killed because of me. I turned to look lovingly at my dead body–less driveway. Yup. I could even go home if I wanted to. There was nothing that tied me to this murder.

Yeah, right. Like I'd go. This whole thing was just too intriguing to pass up.

Unfortunately, half the neighborhood also thought the same as they started stepping out into their yards and walking toward us.

"What's going on?" the little old lady next door asked. Actually, she shouted it. She's deaf but still insisted on talking to everyone. I'd always thought she was faking it, but Rex wouldn't let me use my polygraph equipment on her. That had been followed by a discussion on why I had polygraph equipment.

I shook my head, figuring I'd give her a visual aid to go with what I was going to say, just in case Rex was right. "Murder! Someone killed the pizza guy!"

My shouting drew the attention of the rest of the neighbors, who all started crowding around me, asking more questions.

"Who's the victim?"

"Did you see it happen?"

"Hey! I know that car! Why would anyone kill that nitwit?"

"My pants are too tight!" That one came from the elderly man who lived with the deaf old lady. I was pretty sure it was the only thing he could say because I'd never heard him say anything else in the two years that I'd lived here.

"What's that, Elmer?" his wife shouted.

Elmer responded by unbuttoning his pants and dropping them to the ground. Rex saw it all and sent Kevin over to escort the man back into his house. This caused the crowd to disperse, probably because they couldn't unsee a pantsless Elmer.

"You should go home too," Rex said.

I stared at him. "I wouldn't miss this for the world!"

He shook his head. "For once this investigation isn't tied to you. You're a civilian. You should go home."

"Technically…" I held up a finger. "It does involve me because I was going to eat the pizza this guy delivered."

"Technically," Rex countered, "I can arrest you for interfering if you don't go home."

We stared at each other for a moment before I gave in. I never was any good at stare-offs.

"What about date night?"

The detective looked back at his driveway, which was now crawling with people in white coveralls. He turned back to me with a frown.

"I think date night is off for tonight. Sorry. I'll call you later when everyone's gone."

With an attitude that would rival an angry toddler on a Pixy Stix high, I spun on my heel and went home. At least this time there was no blood to wash off my steps.

CHAPTER TWO

Philby and Martini refused to have anything to do with me, and I felt the best thing to do would be to get out of the house for a bit. It was early still, about 6:00 p.m. If Rex was depriving me of a rented movie, I'd just go out and see a real one.

To be honest, in the two years I'd lived here since I'd moved back, I'd never once been to the movie theatre. Rex and I tended to stay in on date night, usually because making out at a public movie might be frowned upon, and he had a reputation to protect. Actually, that was my excuse. I just liked snuggling during a movie with the cats melted all over us.

I stood numbly before ten movie posters plastered to the outside of a faux-art-deco theatre. There were a lot of choices. Too many choices. In fact I had no idea what any of these movies were about. One had two people kissing—so that must be a romance. Since I wasn't getting any romance tonight, I'd skip that one.

There were a couple of films that looked like romantic comedies and a few horror movies, but I didn't find any of these interesting either. Kelly was always trying to get me to go see what she called chick flicks, but I always turned her down. If I went to one without her, I'd be in serious trouble. And I'd take the CIA being pissed at me over my best friend's wrath any day of the week.

I finally settled on one that looked like a spy thriller. The guy on the poster was sneaking around a dark alley, and the name of the film was *Spy Diary*. It reminded me of the aforementioned night in Qatar, so I picked that one.

After spending what seemed like a week's salary on a ticket, popcorn, pop, and candy, I found a seat in the very back of the auditorium. The lights were already out, and the previews had started.

I tried to focus on the trailers for the eighteenth sequel to this and the twenty-third prequel to that, but my mind began to wander. Who had killed the pizza nitwit? Had he stiffed someone? Was he in the Federal Witness Protection Program? No, that couldn't be right. The feds wouldn't give someone like that a job where they would be in the public eye that much. What if he was a bad guy—sent here to assassinate someone? Pizza delivery guy would be a great cover.

Or maybe he was an undercover cop? He looked pretty young, but that would make him even better at it. But why would an undercover cop be in Rex's driveway? Was he being investigated? I was pretty sure the detective wouldn't like that. Besides, Rex was perfect in every way. There'd be no reason to send an undercover operative to deliver a pizza to him.

At least it didn't have anything to do with me. I gave myself a little mental high five (I really liked high-fiving) and turned my attention back to the screen. The theatre was only about a quarter full, and everyone else was a lot closer to the screen than I. It was kind of like I was the supreme puppet master looking down on the peasants who would do my bidding. Maybe I should've gone for one of the horror flicks. The thought made me laugh.

"Shhhhh!" An angry woman ten rows in front of me glared back at me.

I shrugged and mouthed a little *sorry*. It was just the previews. It wasn't like the movie had started…oh wait. I guess it had. The spy guy was racing down the same alley as pictured in the poster. How much had I missed by daydreaming?

Two guys jumped out in front of him, menacingly— which was pretty much the only way anyone jumped out at you in an alley. You never heard of anyone coming at you *cheerfully* under those circumstances. Been there, done that. Ah, the good old days.

The spy on the screen was backed up against the wall. Oh wow. This was familiar territory for me. It would be fun to see how he got out of this one. Some of these movies were so ridiculous. The hero shoots a guy a mile away with a little handgun and hits his target with more accuracy than a sniper rifle placed up against the target's heart.

Or he ran for forty miles without panting or sweating. Or he went thirty-six hours without eating, sleeping, or even sitting in a chair for a moment. And don't get me started on James Bond. If I ate and drank like he did in the books, I would die. Probably within the first twelve hours.

In reality, spies were human just like everyone else—unless they were Russian. I was pretty sure Russian spies were soulless cyborgs. We bleed, get colds, feel fear, and occasionally think about running away and joining the circus (no one ever shoots the trapeze artist). The movie industry wasn't doing my industry any favors by making us look like superheroes.

Who wrote these movies? Certainly not anyone with any experience as a spy. I thought you kind of needed some experience to write about espionage. How could you write a story about a spy without having once been a spy?

Focus, Merry! You paid like $500 to see this stupid movie! I shook my head to clear it and, once again, looked toward the screen.

Instead, my attention was drawn to a man several rows ahead of me. There was something ridiculously familiar about him. It was pretty dark though. Would I be able to use the light on my cell to see him better? No, that would probably make the woman in front of me implode.

Argh! Now I was seeing things. That was it. I didn't know this guy. Give a spy a murder, and she'll give you a conspiracy to go with it. But then I remembered that this most recent murder had nothing to do with me. That made me ridiculously happy.

The man turned his head to the side as he checked out one of the exits. A very spy move if I ever saw one. Wait...I knew that profile...but the hair was too short. It couldn't be. Could it?

Riley? Was Riley here? Last I'd heard from him, he was on a job in the Middle East. And the only other times Riley had been here were when the Agency wanted him to look in on me. And not in the nice way.

The man turned his head back to the screen, and I squinted into the murky darkness. There was no way I was going to figure out if my former boss was here. Not until the lights went up. Then I'd find out my imagination was running away with me. And it wouldn't be the first time that had happened either.

An explosion rang out from the screen, and I saw that the man in the alley had fired his gun. Why did they have to make the sound so unrealistic? One of the assailants kicked the gun from the spy's hand with a noisy and silly roundhouse kick. Seriously? The roundhouse kick was absurd. You were extremely vulnerable in the time it took you to spin around, and as a result, you couldn't land your blow with enough force. And the impact of a foot hitting a face didn't sound like the crack of a snare drum. There was no sound at all. So why add any? Movies. Right?

The spy jumped over a garbage can and rummaged through it looking for a weapon. Any weapon. I smothered a giggle because I'd once done that too. It was like that story I mentioned about being in Qatar and defending myself with a—

Huh?

The spy in the movie had fished something out of the can and began to defend himself with a wire coat hanger.

I almost dropped my popcorn (thank goodness the pop was in the cup holder—that would've been an expensive tragedy). That was a strange coincidence. I *guess* a writer could've come up with that idea. But what were the odds? It would have definitely been a long shot.

Ugh. Now I was seeing things in movies. I came here to get away from reality. Riley wasn't here, and this movie was just a movie. I settled back into my seat and took a deep breath. In spite of myself, I checked the guy in front. Still there.

What had gotten into me? I was imagining my boss in the front row and was weirded out by a scene in a movie that echoed something that had happened to me. Was this what happened to spies when they retired? They started to see conspiracies around every corner?

Again, I realized I was distracted and tried to focus on the movie. The spy was out of the alley now and stealing across the lawn of a huge mansion in the early twilight of the evening. Ha! I had had a case like that once.

It was in Montenegro. I had infiltrated the home of a gunrunner with a fetish for all things Hawaiian. His house had been filled with palm trees. There had been about a foot of sand on the floor, and his security team had to wear Hawaiian shirts. This guy had even had an entire wall of ukuleles, and I'd ended up smashing a bright purple uke over the head of one of his guards. Maybe I should have started writing this down. I could write a screenplay that would represent my field realistically.

The spy slipped through the door and was immediately greeted by a hallway filled with palm trees, the floor covered with sand.

I'm pretty sure I stopped breathing.

On the screen someone was coming down the hall (I heard the footfall of heavy shoes, which was ridiculous since the floor was covered with sand), so the spy ran into a room filled with tiki gods and…a whole wall of ukuleles. A security guard in a loud Hawaiian shirt came in, and I watched in shock as the spy bludgeoned him with a bright purple ukulele.

When I thought I should write down my past adventures, it'd never occurred to me that someone already had.

CHAPTER THREE

I sat through the movie and watched scene after scene mirror past events of my espionage days. There, in Technicolor for everyone to see, was my encounter with a giant Chechen rebel with a spitting problem, the Hungarian poisoner who'd killed one of my contacts by giving him cyanide-laced bubblegum, and the rather embarrassing episode with an angry howler monkey in Guatemala.

The room was spinning. Okay, it wasn't really spinning. Maybe I was spinning. In any event, I felt like I was going to vomit, scream, or start shooting. My career as a field agent was on this huge screen in my hometown! The only difference was that I was played by a man instead of a woman—which was kind of skeevy.

Who had made this movie? Who had written it? And why?

A new thought chilled me even more. Did the CIA think I'd spilled my guts to Hollywood? That was a *huge* no-no. Virtually all of these scenes were from cases that were still classified. And yet, here they were for all of America to see.

With blood pounding in my veins, I turned on my cell and did an internet search of the movie. It had just opened. Tonight. All across the country.

The movie was unexpectedly shut off, and the house lights came up. The crowd started to complain as a middle-aged man came in and introduced himself as the manager. In a nervous voice, he explained that the film had been inadvertently destroyed, and we'd all get our money back. The man was sweating profusely. And he was lying.

My eyes darted to the front of the theatre. People were already filing out toward the lobby, grumbling. The guy who looked like Riley wasn't there. I exited the movie theatre, but instead of getting my money back, ran to my car and locked myself in.

"Maria," I said after I was able to call her number with shaking hands.

"Merry," she whispered. "Call you in five." The call ended.

I sat there in my car, staring at the poster on the front of the building. It took a little while to slow my breathing—I was badly shaken. A few minutes later, I watched the same sweaty manager take the poster down. After looking both ways he walked around the side of the building and tossed it into a dumpster.

I waited until he'd gone back inside before I retrieved it and drove home at about eighty miles per hour (which, in a small town, means I was back at my house in two minutes). I was in the door and had unrolled the poster on the breakfast counter when Maria called back.

"I just saw it!" I didn't wait for her to say anything. "For the first time in two years, I go to a movie. And see my whole career on the screen! What's happening?"

"So you know..." Maria's voice had a hint of worry.

"Just now! The manager shut it down halfway through and tossed the poster in the trash. I'm looking at it right now!"

"So you didn't know," Maria said a little more confidently. Apparently, that was the answer she'd wanted to hear.

I shook my head, even though she couldn't see me. "I had no idea! Who made this movie? And how? Those cases are all classified!"

"I haven't seen it," Maria said. "But I guess the deputy director took his kids to see the matinee. The word has spread."

It felt like I'd suddenly shrunk about five sizes. "The deputy director?" My voice cracked a little. "Why would he take his kids to that movie? It's PG-13!" Granted, kids are more mature these days, and maybe I'm overreacting, but it seemed like a bad decision.

"Everyone's talking about it." She hesitated. "Everyone's talking about *you*."

Why couldn't I just retire like all the other normal spies? You know, play golf or knit? One woman even joined the Somali pirates. Of course, no one had heard from her since...

"It was just a random thing," I said. "I never go to the movies, and all the other movies looked stupid. It's pure chance that I was even there."

My tingly spy-dey senses kicked in, and I started racing around my little ranch house, locking doors and closing curtains. Now where was my gun?

"Merry!" Maria's voice reminded me that I was still on the phone.

"Oh! Sorry!" I slammed the kitchen window shut and turned the lock.

I'd need to buy a professional security system. I should've done so a while ago, but I thought my life was finally going to be wonderfully boring. I opened my laptop and started looking for local businesses that could hook me up.

"Merry!" Maria sounded angry. "Have you heard anything that I just said?"

"Um, sure," I lied. "But, maybe because I'm a little freaked out, you could tell me again?"

There was a sigh of exasperation that I'd heard a million times before, mostly from Riley.

"This is bad, Merry. They think you did it."

"Did what?" I asked, my mind racing.

"They think you leaked the intel. They think you wrote the screenplay or something. And, Merry?" There was a pause here as I imagined her looking around to make sure she wasn't overheard.

"They're coming for you."

CHAPTER FOUR

Once I regained the use of my voice, I asked, "Is Riley here? In Who's There?"

Maria sounded confused. "What? No. Not that I'm aware of."

"I thought I saw him in the theatre. I can't be sure. His hair was shorter. But I could swear it was him. Unfortunately, I lost him."

I heard the clicking of computer keys. "No, he's still out of the country."

She couldn't tell me where he was, and I was fine with that. I'd gotten her in trouble with her superiors more than once before.

"Okay. Thanks for the heads-up. Any idea who they'll send?"

"No. I'll text you from my personal cell when I know," Maria said quietly before hanging up.

She was so amazing. I didn't warrant that kind of loyalty. Maria Gomez had helped me take my Girl Scout troop to Washington, DC in the summer. That alone qualified her for canonization for the next five lifetimes.

So here's what I knew. Someone had told my life story to someone in Hollywood, and they'd made a movie out of it. I looked at the poster. Both Philby and Martini were sitting on it, looking at me meaningfully.

"This is ridiculous," I muttered as I gave them each a little plate of tuna. "I can't figure out how this happened."

The cats devoured the meat as if they'd hunted and killed it themselves, and looked to me for more, but I wasn't falling for it. I probably shouldn't have even given them that. Philby had a very sensitive stomach and could, at any time…

The cat belched loudly before barfing on the poster-spy's face.

"I know what you mean," I said as I got a roll of paper towels out and cleaned it up. "I feel the same way."

The clock on the stove told me it was too late to call Rex. That was okay because I had no idea what I'd say to him. Telling him would be a violation of the confidentiality clause I'd signed when I'd retired. On the other hand, half the country had just seen part of, if not all of the movie, so we were sort of in a gray area.

I picked up my cell and called Riley. He was the only person I could safely talk to.

"This is Riley. Leave a message."

I should've seen that coming. He was working. Bothering him was not a good idea. What was up with his doppelganger at the movie theatre? Maybe Riley knew about the movie—I looked at the poster—*Spy Diary*. It literally was a diary…mine. If I'd been allowed to keep a diary that is.

It could have been that he was here to find out if I had leaked classified information. But why would I do that? Riley knew I wouldn't. I was a consummate professional. I'd never betray the Agency. Never. Plus, I didn't want some "cleaner" to show up on my doorstep with a pair of pliers and duct tape to remind me how confidentiality clauses worked. And yes, there is a guy who does that. His name is Rueben.

Not knowing what else to do, I hung the poster on the fridge. I had to displace some Girl Scout Council info to do so. Staring at the papers, I realized I'd totally forgotten about a troop meeting in the morning. We were going to discuss some upcoming camp fund-raiser. Kelly had invited someone from the Council to join us.

It had better not be Juliette Dowd. That low-level bimbo hated me just because she and Rex had dated once. No, Kelly was my best friend. She'd make sure it was someone else. The rest of the staff was awesome. Amazing really. First-rate professionals who made me wonder why they'd hired an angry woman like Juliette.

With a yawn, I stretched and decided to hit the hay. Sleeping when I might be under surveillance didn't terrify me nearly as much as not being totally ready for a troop meeting. When it came to my girls, the CIA looked like declawed, narcoleptic kittens.

* * *

"Mrs. Wrath!" The four Kaitlyns slammed into me with a group hug. I had four girls named Kaitlyn in my troop. And they each spelled their names differently. And they all had brown hair and *M* as the initial for their last name. I never could tell them apart. It was an impossible task, like teaching a chicken to read.

"Hey, guys!" I croaked as I was crushed between them.

I had to put aside my worries that the CIA would barge in and drag me off at any moment. Well, that and I'd surveilled the school three times before the meeting.

"Okay, ladies!" Kelly held up her right hand in the Scout sign for silence.

The Kaitlyns found their seats with the other girls. It always worked. I had no idea why.

"This is Mrs. Conrad." She pointed to a smiling, thirtysomething woman in a green sweater and scarf covered in the Scout logo. "She's going to talk about the camp fund-raiser."

The lady handed out flyers and said, "We're going to have a mud run at Camp Singing Bird this year! It'll be an obstacle course, and teams will be competing with each other to win the grand prize."

Lauren's hand shot up into the air. "What's the grand prize?"

Mrs. Conrad smiled. I liked her immediately. I liked all of the Council staff really. Except for Juliette, but there wasn't anything I could do about that. The rest of them were wonderful, warm, funny women. Adults, I got. Kids, I was still learning about.

"The grand prize is a weekend camping trip to Camp North Star!"

Oohs and aahs filled the air. Camp North Star was a big deal. Located close to the Mississippi River, that camp had more than most, with indoor/outdoor pools, a high-ropes course, climbing walls, zip lines, a lazy river to tube on, a mud pit with mudslide, and horses. Everyone knew about Camp North Star. And groups of all kinds wanted to go there for camping or team building...stuff like that.

My troop of third-grade girls would do anything to camp at North Star, and I'd planned to take them next summer...if I could. It was hard to get in and usually booked one year out. But winning this competition seemed like an easy way to make it happen.

"Well," Betty said matter-of-factly, "we're going to win."

Mrs. Conrad nodded. "It wouldn't surprise me at all if you did!"

I liked how she didn't patronize the girls. She took their interests seriously. That was nice. Maybe I should try that.

"Review the information and have your leaders fill out the necessary forms. I will see you in a few weeks!"

Kelly walked the Scout official out to the parking lot, and I studied the form. The contest would take place in late September. Not bad. The weather would be nice—in the 70s at least.

"Mrs. Wrath?" Hannah (one of two in my troop) asked. No matter how many times I told the girls I wasn't married, they still insisted on calling me *Mrs.* "You will fill out the forms, won't you?"

My jaw dropped. "When have I ever let you down?"

The girls looked at each other a little too long for my comfort.

"Of course we're going!" I insisted. "And you're right, Betty—we're going to win."

I left out the part where I might be at CIA HQ in Langley, where I'd face the equivalent of a court-martial for treason. My stomach knotted up at the thought of it.

Kelly rejoined us and got the girls involved in a craft activity making autumn leaves out of construction paper. School had just started, and the girls appeared to be happy. Of course they were. Elementary school rocked. How could you not be happy coloring with crayons and having two recesses a day?

"I don't know if I can make it." Kelly frowned at the flyer. "I'm supposed to take Finn to see my parents in Omaha. It's a family reunion." Finn was her baby daughter. Named after me, or my real name, that is. Finnoughla. I loved that little girl, but now she was infringing on my shot at Camp North Star.

"What? You're joking. Tell me you're joking."

She shook her head. "I'll help you get ready, and I'll find someone to replace me on the day of the mud run. But I really can't go."

"You can't go, Mrs. Albers?" Lauren asked in horror.

Apparently, the girls had heard. This was not unusual as they had the hearing of bionic bats. Sometimes I swear they heard things from two buildings away. And on one occasion, I was pretty sure they'd bugged my house.

"I'm sorry," Kelly said sadly. "But we have family members flying in from Seattle and Florida. They've already gotten their tickets. I can't change all that."

Lauren and Betty started a huddle that included all twelve girls in attendance. We watched them for a few moments until they seemed to agree on something. One of the Kaitlyns stood up.

"Okay. We want Dr. Body to go with us."

The other girls nodded. I was a bit less than thrilled. But the girls had visited the morgue once and were completely in the woman's thrall.

"She ran cross-country and track in college," Hannah Number One added. "And she looks like a jock."

Looks like a jock? The woman stole two of my cats! I thought about telling the girls that Dr. Body was too pretty to go on a mud run, but was interrupted.

"That's a great idea!" Kelly agreed. She pulled out her cell and called.

"Shouldn't we talk about this?" I said quietly. "Maybe there's someone else better?"

My best friend shot me a look that told me to shut up, albeit politely. Kelly didn't put up with any crap from me, which was one of the reasons I loved her. With the exception of this very moment, that is.

"Soo Jin?" Kelly smiled. She always smiled when she talked to the coroner. Did she smile when she talked to me on the phone? Mental note: plant hidden cameras in Kelly's house. I should keep an eye on my goddaughter anyway.

I watched helplessly as she talked to the doctor. I really needed to get over my anger toward her. Dr. Body was a nice person. Even I disgruntledly liked her. Maybe I could do this and show Kelly that I was an adult and a worthy godmother to Finn.

"She's in!" Kelly put her cell away, and the girls cheered enthusiastically before going back to making paper leaves.

"We should've talked about this first," I grumbled.

"Why?" Kelly asked before walking over to the tables to supervise.

"Because there are two of us? Because we're co-leaders?" I retorted as I followed her over.

Ava, Inez, and Caterina, who were usually quiet, were fighting each other with glue sticks.

"Whoa!" I bent down to the table and retrieved the weapons. "What's going on here?"

Ava sighed. "Inez said that Dr. Body will beat you in the mud run. Caterina and I think she's wrong."

I wanted to take a moment and revel in their faith. Maybe even high-five the girls. But that would be the wrong reaction. I think.

"We will all have to work together as a team. Everyone on the team will score points that, added together, will give us our team score." At least, I thought that was how it would work.

"We need to start training," Betty shouted from the next table, which was a bit much since she was right next to me.

"Good idea!" Hannah Number One said. Hannah Number Two agreed. "Can we go out there next weekend and practice?"

I shrugged. It seemed like a good idea. Get the drop on the other troops. But maybe it wasn't fair to do that? As a spy, I would've started setting it up already. But as a leader, I was pretty sure it wasn't sportsmanlike.

Kelly—ever the adult—intervened. "No, we can't do that. But maybe we can train to work together as a team."

"I know!" Caterina jumped up. "We can play laser tag!"

A chorus of enthusiastic cries filled the air.

"At that place by the mall!" Inez said. "I love it there!"

"What's laser tag?" I asked.

Shrill screams buzzed in our ears. The girls all started shouting over each other in an attempt to explain to me what laser tag is.

"So you shoot people?" I asked with probably more enthusiasm than necessary.

"With lasers." Betty nodded. "Everyone wears a vest with things on them that tell you if you've been hit."

"And it's dark in the room," Lauren added. "But we need a team to practice against."

One of the Kaitlyns raised her hand. "We could play against my brother's Boy Scout troop. I'd love to kick Brian's butt."

The girls decided that this was the plan before Kelly or I could even respond.

"Boy Scouts, eh?" I smiled. "I love it! How soon can it be arranged?"

Kaitlyn shrugged. "Mom will be here soon. I'll ask her. Dad's their leader."

The matter was settled, and the girls went back to their crafts.

"I'm not sure this is a good idea," Kelly whispered. "I think it sends the wrong message to the girls with all that shooting."

I ignored her because I was pulling up information about laser tag on my cell. After reading about it online, I only loved the idea more.

"The girls have decided." I shrugged.

"Yeah, but..." Kelly started to say.

I pointed at her. "You said you wanted the girls to start taking more initiative in planning events."

Kelly once again tried to speak, but I stopped her.

"You said that. And you also said the girls needed to bond more. This is perfect."

"I don't know," Kelly muttered as the first of the moms arrived to pick up their girls.

We waited with the Kaitlyn with the brother named Brian until her mother showed up. I was still on high alert that the Agency could show up out of the blue, but I had a laser tag game to plan, and that trumped all other fears.

Ashley (all of the Kaitlyns' moms were named Ashley—something I believe they did on purpose to cause confusion) agreed that this was a good idea and said she'd set it up for the next day. Kelly started to protest that she had a prior commitment, but Ashley said the boys were getting together in the afternoon anyway, so we might as well get it over with. She left, and the girls were all gone.

Kelly didn't say anything as she started putting the craft supplies away. I decided to try a different subject.

"So...have you heard from Riley?"

Kelly loved my former boss so much that he was the godfather to my being godmother. If he was in town, she'd probably know about it.

"No. Isn't he on a mission or something?" she said as she handed me a box of glue sticks.

"He's supposed to be. But I could swear I saw him at the movies last night."

Kelly stared at me. "You went to the movies? Since when do you go out? Did you go with Rex? Why didn't you ask me?"

"You always want to see those romance movies." I shuddered.

"Yeah, but I'd go see anything at this point." Kelly bit her lip.

"What are you talking about?"

She shrugged. "I need to get out of the house more. Robert needs to do more with the baby. I'm going a little stir-crazy."

I hadn't thought of that. I guess I assumed that new parents wanted to spend every moment hanging on every breath their baby breathed.

"Everything is fine." My best friend waved me off. "Tell me why you think you saw Riley."

I filled her in on the dead pizza guy and my trip to the theatre. I left out the bit about the movie being a dead ringer for my life. I still wasn't sure exactly how classified that was.

She shook her head. "I can't see Riley cutting his hair. Ever. And if he was in town, he'd call. Right?"

"I guess so…"

"So don't worry about it." She picked up her bag and two boxes. "I've got to get home to Finn. I'll let Soo Jin know about the laser tag competition tomorrow and reschedule my meeting at work. I'll pick you up at two. Okay?"

I nodded and followed her out. We both lived on the same block as the elementary school, and I usually walked over. But Kelly had all those boxes, so she had driven. We stashed the stuff in the trunk of her car, and I waved as she drove off.

Whether I liked it or not, Dr. Body and I were going to be partners. I'd have to suspend my irrational dislike for her and move on. And right then I needed to see that laser tag range. They might not let us onto the mud run course at camp, but that wouldn't stop me from surveilling the location of the game the next day.

* * *

"Ma'am." The teenager who ran the laser tag arena squeaked as he talked, his Adam's apple bobbing. A large plastic nametag said *Trent.* "There's no one playing right now. I can't let you into the room unless you are playing."

I handed him a twenty. "There, now I'm paying. Which means I want to play."

"But you're alone," the kid protested. "How can you play against yourself?"

I thought about this for a moment. "I'll play you."

"Me?" He was a skinny kid with shoulder-length hair and braces. "I'm working!"

"Do you take breaks?" I asked as I pulled another twenty dollar bill out and waved it at him.

He looked around. It was quiet. The arena was part of a huge entertainment complex, and most people were in the bowling alley. This whole complex was definitely more than Who's There needed.

"I can put a sign on the door," he said slowly, the wheels turning inside his head. "Closed for maintenance. My boss never comes round on the weekends."

I held up another twenty. "I don't care how you justify it. I just want to see how it works."

Trent shrugged. "Okay." He put a sign up and then opened the door.

We walked into a room that had row upon row of what looked to be vests and belts with holsters. Trent put on a vest and strapped on his laser gun. He then helped me into mine and showed me how to use it.

According to Trent, the room was set up to mirror a little bombed-out village. There were walls with windows, fake rock formations, doors, etc. You had to shoot someone point-blank in the chest to score a hit. I was a little disappointed that that was all. I expected the victim to get shocked with electricity or something.

"Every ten minutes, you have to go to the wall on your side of the room and put your gun in a hole that's lit up. That recharges it. The game ends when a team scores fifty points. The lights will come on when that happens, ending the game."

That sounded reasonable. Trent went through a weapons check with me and opened the door.

"I'll go to the far side since you haven't been here before." Gone was the squeaky, nervous voice, and in its place was a steady, calm demeanor.

I decided I'd try to go easy on him. After all, I had real field experience. This kid wouldn't know what had hit him. I intended to win and was pretty sure it would take only a few minutes for me to hit fifty.

I couldn't have been more wrong. The minute we were plunged into a dim darkness, Trent turned from a nervous wreck into Liam Neeson. Various things glowed in the dark to give you some light. Every time I turned around, I saw the little gleam of red from his pistol. My vest went off so many times that I worried that I might actually explode. At one point I actually hoped the CIA would barge in and drag me away.

It felt like I was constantly recharging my gun. At least the charging port was a safe place where he couldn't get me. As far as I knew, I hadn't hit him even once. There had to be something wrong with my gun.

This kid was like an invisible spider monkey. Every time I thought I knew where he was, he surprised me and shot me before summoning his invisibility superpowers and vanishing into thin air. The lights came on after ten minutes. Trent had smoked me. I didn't know what had hit me.

"Not bad," Trent said as he collected our gear and hung it up on the wall. "I guess it's a good thing you're not a cop or a spy or something." His high-pitched laughter caused his Adam's apple to bob in a frenzy.

"Well," I said grudgingly, "I was just trying to get the lay of the land before tomorrow. We're going up against a Boy Scout team."

Trent's eyes grew wide. "Not Brian Miller's team! He's got the highest score of anyone here, even me!"

"I'm sure he's not that good." My heart sank. It had to be Kaitlyn's brother. How many Brian M's were Boy Scouts?

Trent whistled. "Well, good luck. I'm sorry I won't be here tomorrow to watch."

I tried not to smile. At least I wouldn't have this stupid kid gloating over us.

Wait… "Watch?"

He nodded. "We have cameras in there so that we can watch to make sure no one gets too rough."

"Do they record?" The last thing I needed was for this to get out.

"No. Maybe someday." Trent led me through the door and removed the sign.

Our game was over, and so was our conversation, as he became a nervous teen all over again. I grumbled all the way out to the car. On the way home I decided to spend the rest of the day googling laser tag cheats.

If Brian the Boy Scout was as good as Trent seemed to think he was, we were totally screwed.

CHAPTER FIVE

Rex knocked on my door the next day at one o'clock in the afternoon. With a quick kiss and the mandatory adoration required by Philby (who was upset from the fresh hell of another pill dosing), Rex settled in on the couch. Martini and Philby jumped into his lap and were asleep in seconds. My boyfriend could magically induce instant catatonic states in cats. I seemed to electrify them because they ran from room to room as if they were on fire whenever I came near them.

"What's up with the dead guy in *your* driveway?" I asked as I started to stretch. I enjoyed the little rush of happiness that came with the words *your driveway*.

Rex watched as I reached both arms over my head and bent over at the waist until my fingers brushed the floor. This wasn't easy to do because I had no flexibility whatsoever. But I forced it because I didn't want to look…um…inflexible in front of my guy. And it hurt. I'd definitely be feeling that tomorrow.

"His name was Dewey Barnes. He was a part-time pizza guy and part-time marijuana dealer." His right eyebrow arched as I started running in place with my knees almost meeting my chest. Another thing that was usually impossible for me to do. I would be so stiff from trying to impress Rex that I would probably be mainlining ibuprofen within the hour.

"So he has a record?" I attempted to ask through my panting, which was alarming. I was seriously out of shape. Maybe I could take Philby running. Did people jog with cats? I tried to imagine that, but all I could come up with was me dragging an angry cat that looked like Hitler through my neighborhood.

He shook his head. "Nothing. He moved here two years ago from Des Moines, where he grew up. College dropout, not a lot of friends or hobbies, and as far as I can see, no evidence of anyone who'd want to kill him."

I stopped running and stretched my right arm up and over my left side. I was rewarded with a searing pain that told me I was probably going to die from stretching.

"That's weird. We don't get random shootings here."

Rex stared at me as I did the other side. "What are you doing?"

I filled him in on the laser tag match scheduled to take place at right about the time all the pain from stretching would kick in. He probably knew nothing about laser tag. And why would he? Rex didn't strike me as the type who played games with kids.

"Brian Miller? *The* Brian Miller?" Rex looked impressed.

"Yes," I said with more than a little irritation. "You know him?"

"No, but I've definitely heard of him. He's won the Iowa State Laser Tag Championship four years in a row. They say he'll go to nationals this year."

I stopped stretching because it seemed a bit pointless now and everything hurt. "Really? That's a thing?"

Rex nodded. "There's not a lot that goes on here. Don't you read the paper?"

My gaze traveled to the pile of unopened, rolled-up newspapers in the corner behind the door. I was saving them for a campfire. Rex spotted the newspapers.

"I guess not," he said with a grin. "I wish I wasn't working this afternoon. Your troop taking on Brian Miller would be something to watch."

I narrowed my eyes. "It's just a training exercise with my girls. The most important thing will be that we bond."

I didn't really believe that. In the back of my mind was the constant worry that the CIA would show up at the entertainment center with *real* guns. But Maria hadn't texted, so I figured I was safe—at least for today. And I wanted to focus on crushing the Boy Scouts. I wanted to destroy this Brian Miller.

"Well, good luck." Rex got up and pulled me into a lovely kiss.

"Oh, ye of little faith," I said as I pushed away and opened the front door, indicating he should go.

Soo Jin was standing in the doorway when I opened it. She broke into a smile at seeing us.

"Hey, guys!" Dr. Body bounced into the room, looking adorable with her silky, black hair in a high ponytail, wearing a tight gym shirt that said *Yale* and tiny shorts to match.

"She's helping you?" Rex asked with a grin. "Maybe you'll have half a chance."

He said good-bye to me and the coroner, and I shut the door while cursing him under my breath. Philby and Martini came running from the hallway and started rubbing against Soo Jin's perfect legs. She responded by dropping to the floor and running her fingers over their fur. The purring was so loud that it could probably be heard by Rex across the street.

The traitors.

A honk sounded outside. I grabbed my purse and Soo Jin, dragging her out to Kelly's car. My best friend greeted the doctor with a little more enthusiasm than I thought was necessary.

"You've got shotgun, Soo Jin!" Kelly patted the seat beside her.

It took all of my strength to not roll my eyes. To be honest, I was a little proud of myself. Instead I just grumbled in my own head as we made our way through town.

The girls were waiting for us when we pulled into the parking lot.

"Did I miss something?" I asked Kelly. "Why are they dressed up?"

Each one of my Scouts was wearing a dress. Some had bows in their hair. They never looked like that. In fact, I couldn't think of one time since I'd known these kids that they had ever dressed up.

"Brian's troop must be hotties," Soo Jin said.

Is that what this was about? These were eight- and nine-year-olds! And how could we hope to compete at the mud run if they dressed like that? Clearly the girls weren't taking this seriously. Maybe there was an army surplus store around here where I could buy them all tactical gear.

"Here we go." Kelly parked the car, and we herded the girls to the spot where I'd been spanked by a kid only twenty-four hours earlier.

"Hi." A slightly older teenage boy smiled as we walked up. "I'm Alex."

Alex was a good-looking kid. Really good-looking. Too good-looking. And confident. I noticed my girls staring openmouthed at him. Maybe Alex was who they had dressed up for?

"Trent told me you were coming." Alex smiled warmly, and the four Kaitlyns melted. Yup. The troop was trying to impress Alex. That was a relief. I didn't want them to throw the match because they wanted to flirt with Brian's troop.

"Let's get you guys suited up before the boys get here. Okay?" Alex winked. Inez and Caterina swooned.

Once we were decked out in our tech vests, I couldn't help but laugh. The girls looked like they were going to a combination birthday party/terrorist conflict. I watched the two Hannahs practice quick draws from their holsters, and Betty was working on a menacing grimace while Inez threw punches at one of the Kaitlyn's outstretched palms.

"Does this look strange to you?" Kelly leaned toward me.

I nodded. "Totally." Now this was the troop I knew! "These little boys are going down."

"You mean those little boys?" Kelly pointed.

I looked to see a platoon of high school–aged boys approaching us. Many of them were taller than me, and all of them were taller than my girls. They wore their uniforms (which I thought was weird), and more than a few had camo-painted faces.

"Hey!" I said to the Kaitlyns. "You didn't say they were so old!"

Soo Jin whistled under her breath. But when the boys saw her, they stopped dead, eyes bulging. Maybe we had an advantage after all.

One of the Kaitlyns stepped forward as the other girls formed a line behind her. "Hello, Brian. Ready to get your butt kicked?"

A tall boy, who seemed to be part redwood tree, stepped forward and taunted. "You guys are toast. This match will be over in minutes, and I'm not going to buy you ice cream when you cry like a baby."

To her credit, Brian's little sister stepped up, pointing at him. "When we win, you have to post on Facebook and Instagram that you got schooled by Girl Scouts."

Brian sneered at his sister, and the other boys chuckled. "Is this your troop? You'll need an army to defeat us."

For a brief moment I toyed with calling a friend of mine in the Navy SEALs who owed me a favor. I'd like to see Brian wet himself when approached by ten giant men with tattoos and sniper rifles. Sadly, there wasn't enough time.

Betty stepped forward. "Eat it, douchebag!"

"Betty!" Kelly shouted. I was actually impressed that Betty knew what a douchebag was.

The girl looked at her, made what might've been a gang sign, then spun on her heel and rejoined the group. What was happening here? Why didn't I know these boys were mutants? And why did these boys laugh at little girls? I wanted to run back to my house for my hidden stash of CIA-grade LSD tabs (I might've taken one or two office supplies with me when I left the Agency) to shove down these boys' throats. If we were going to lose, they might as well have been hallucinating that we were rabid dragons or at least giant, menacing butterflies.

"Don't go crying to your mama when you lose!" Brian barked. I wondered if he remembered that Kaitlyn's mama was also his own. This family seemed to have a bizarre dynamic.

"You're going down!" his sister shouted.

Then, as suddenly as it had started, the posturing ended. A smiling man emerged from behind the wall of mutant boys, stepping forward, hand extended.

"Hi-de-ho! I'm Bart Miller. The leader of these boys and Kaitlyn's daddy!"

I shook his hand, briefly considering throwing him to the ground. "Merry Wrath. And this is Kelly Albers. We're the leaders of your daughter's troop."

Bart smiled. "Okeydokey!" He grinned like a dad from a bad 1950s sitcom. "Alrighty, then, boys! Let's get suited up!" Who was this guy? A total happy-go-lucky nerd who didn't realize his troop was planning to slaughter little kids? I guess I'd expected Arnold Schwarzenegger or, at the very least, Vincent Price.

I watched as the guys put on their gear. Every now and then, one of my little girls would stick her tongue out at the boys. Betty actually drew her finger across her throat, but I don't think they were intimidated. Which is too bad because, if they knew Betty, they should have been worried.

"Come here, guys." I pulled Soo Jin and the girls around me into a huddle. "We need a strategy." Hell, we needed a miracle. Or Liam Neeson riding a unicorn.

"Well…" Inez thought out loud. "I think we should cheat."

Caterina nodded. "I brought some pepper spray." She produced a large canister that Kelly confiscated immediately. I thought that was unnecessary of my co-leader. We needed every advantage we could find.

"It's twelve to twelve," Soo Jin said. "I think we can take them."

I liked her enthusiasm, although I worried that she was blind and hadn't actually seen the boys.

"These guys are champions," Kelly said. "We'll need to do something unorthodox just to try to keep up."

I nodded. "Absolutely."

"I brought my dad's brass knuckles." Lauren produced a weapon that I was pretty sure was illegal. Kelly took that away too.

"We can't kill them." Kelly narrowed her eyes at me. That woman could read my mind.

"Did you bring your gun?" Emily asked me. The other girls nodded.

I shook my head. "I really should have…"

"No, you shouldn't have!" Kelly hissed. "Girls! You have to concentrate!"

"It's time!" Alex called out. He opened the door to the little fake city, and we all filed inside.

He went over the rules, and I was relieved to see that the girls were listening carefully. The boys just rolled their eyes while pointing and laughing at them. My hands formed into fists more than once.

"I should've at least brought a stun gun," I said quietly to Soo Jin.

The good coroner giggled loudly. It was charming. It also distracted them, as it reminded the boys of the goddess in tight clothes in their midst. All twelve stopped listening to Alex and more than a few started drooling.

I looked around at the ruins of the fake city, and it hit me.

"Do we get a few minutes to consult our troops?" I blurted out.

Alex looked at me then at Brian, who'd taken to smacking his fist into the palm of his hand. He nodded. "Mrs. Albers and I will be in the observation room watching on hidden cameras. So, boys, I expect a clean match with no picking on the girls."

The boys looked at each other and laughed menacingly. I was pretty sure they weren't going to follow Alex's directive.

I bent down to one knee and said very quietly to my troop, "I have an idea…"

Soon we had taken up positions on our respective sides, and then the lights went out. In the dim room, a dozen little girls looked at me and smiled. The game was on.

CHAPTER SIX

It was a simple plan really. The girls called it Operation Sparkly Killer Pony Princess. Every window or sight line in the burned-out-village-themed room started at about five feet off the ground. My girls were shorter than that.

Three groups of four girls would just walk under the sight line of the windows, turn the corner, and shoot whatever boy was on the other side. Repeatedly. With probably more enthusiasm than was necessary. Then they'd march on to the next barricade and do it again. And again. And again.

The boys never realized what was going on because they were too stupid, or it never occurred to them that just out of the line of sight, a squad of third-graders was sneaking up on them. Actually, they didn't have to sneak at all. Not one of my girls had to stoop to stay undercover.

More than once I heard a boy swear. This was usually followed by their leader chastising them with a "nopey dopey!" The guys couldn't figure out how the girls appeared out of nowhere all of the time. It was a great psychological game. Sigh. I missed the CIA.

Soo Jin had Brian duty. And by that I mean she just shadowed him. If he was about to nail any of my girls, she'd appear, smiling at him until he was so flustered that he didn't realize she'd just shot him forty times. One of her more inspired moves was to fake a fall. Without thinking, Brian helped her up, only to discover too late that she'd shot him as he gave her his hand. I wanted to name this Operation Brian's Glands, but the doctor already had a rough time with the idea of flirting with a kid. So I kept that name to myself.

As for me, I was the gunrunner. Technically speaking, each player was supposed to charge their own gun when they ran out of lasers or whatever it was. Instead, each girl had one gun—but I'd secretly snagged a few more. I followed them, and as soon as they ran out of…um…lasers, I'd take the empty gun and give them one fully loaded.

Every now and then I'd have to run back and reload a bunch of guns, but we timed it just right so that no one was out of ammo. I wasn't sure where the hidden cameras were, but I thought that a couple of times I heard Kelly and Alex laughing. I couldn't be sure. Just as I couldn't be sure that I saw Betty doing something to a boy that involved a little crackle of electricity and him screaming in pain. I can't watch everyone all the time, now can I?

It wasn't long before the lights came on, and the voice of the handsome Alex came over the loudspeakers.

"We have a winner! Congratulations, girls! You won with a score of 50–13!"

Brian had to be restrained as he lunged at his sister. Kaitlyn stood, unflinching, and flicked him hard on the nose.

"Maybe you girls should go take off your gear first," the boys' leader said cheerfully. "And thanks for the super-duper game!"

I didn't wait for a demand for a rematch and began herding everyone into the tech room. We were out in the lobby before the boys came through. To their credit, the girls stood solemnly to the side as the boys emerged, red-faced and humiliated.

"You cheated!" Brian squeaked. His swagger had abandoned him.

Kaitlyn and Brian's mother, Ashley, stepped forward and glared at her son. "I guess you'll have to do dishes for a week for being a bad loser."

Brian's eyes grew wide with fear. Was that all it took? I should've used that threat against the drug runners who'd tried to shoot me in Colombia.

"Mom!" he whined.

The other boys were too deflated to give him a hard time. They left as quickly as they'd arrived. Bart gave us a friendly smile as he herded the boys outside.

"That was awesome!" Alex said as he high-fived each and every girl. More than one gazed at the hand that had touched his with awe. "Normally I'd call you on the gun-charging thing, but you were up against some pretty steep odds."

Kelly grinned widely. "We recorded that." She held up a camcorder. "I'm not sure what we should do with it, but I figure it doesn't hurt to have a little backup ammo."

"I'm not too proud of my part," Soo Jin said. "But those boys got what they deserved."

I didn't tell her that we had to win by any means necessary. My guess was that she wouldn't understand it. Still, I made a mental note to make it up to her. Dr. Body had been a real team player.

The entertainment center was much more crowded when we came out. Late afternoon on a Saturday, I guess. People of all ages were milling about, buying tokens, heading to the game room, or bowling. A line was forming near us for the laser-tag scenario.

A flash of blond caught my eye, and I froze. At the other end of the lobby, I thought I saw Riley. I started to wade through the mass of people. It was only brief glimpses of a nose or chin or those blue eyes, but putting them all together in my mind created a picture of Riley.

Still, I couldn't get a good look. Was it really him? If it was and he hadn't let me know he was in town, I was going to clock him good. Okay, so I'd been mad the past few times he'd shown up unannounced, but this was different. It felt like he was keeping me in the dark.

By the time I reached the other side, Riley—or the man who looked like him—was gone. I kept working my way back and forth across the room but never saw him again.

"What are you doing?" Kelly asked once I'd rejoined them.

"I thought I saw Riley," I whispered.

Kelly frowned and scanned our surroundings. "I don't see him. Are you sure?" I could tell that she was also upset that he may have been here and not said hi.

I shrugged. "I thought so."

Kelly stopped looking around. "I'm sure you're imagining it."

Alex appeared in front of me. "That was amazing. You guys did a great job! After Trent had told me about yesterday, I was sure you were going to get creamed. Man, you girls have guts!"

The girls started cheering. They'd never looked so happy. Even Soo Jin had to laugh. We all went outside and waited for them to get picked up. Once the last girl was gone, Kelly, Soo Jin, and I climbed into the car.

Kelly turned to me. "That really was amazing."

Soo Jin nodded. "You should've been a spy or a general or something."

I tried to look humble. I really did. "I guess I missed my calling."

* * *

"You did *what*?" Rex met up with me at home, holding a large pepperoni pizza.

I poured myself a glass of wine and handed him a beer. "It was easy. Just a matter of physics."

"Physics?" Rex asked. "I'm not sure you understand what physics is."

"Well, proportion, then. Frankly, it was lucky that the windows in the ruins were so high. I don't know if the boys have figured out what happened yet, but I'm pretty sure we can't pull that again."

"Dr. Body was an asset." Rex winked. "I'll bet she wasn't happy about being objectified."

"Speaking of bodies, tell me about your dead guy." I changed the subject and shoved a slice of pizza into my mouth.

My boyfriend rolled his eyes. "Fine. It's going to be on the news tonight anyway. Dewey Barnes was murdered with a small caliber pistol at extremely close range. One bullet did it.

And we did find something interesting in his car. Which is why I'm really here."

I felt the blood drain out of my face. "I don't like the sound of that."

Rex nodded. "We found a map in the glove compartment along with a .45."

I shook my head. "Oh no. You can't pin this on me."

"The map had your address on it. It seems that Dewey was looking for you."

I stomped around like an enraged toddler. "It's not fair! This is *your* dead body! Not mine! Someone planted that to implicate me! Maybe it was Juliette Dowd!"

Oh, I could just see that. My arch nemesis at the Council, Juliette, would do anything to get rid of me so that she could have Rex to herself. Maybe Rex would believe me and arrest her. I wondered if he'd let me ride along for that.

"It wasn't Juliette. And I don't know the significance of the map and gun yet. Barnes has no serious priors. No record of anything other than drug possession, and even then, it was a small amount."

"This murder isn't about me!" I insisted. "It's your turn!"

Rex laughed, "Are you saying I deserve a murder more than you?"

I nodded vigorously. "That's right. Well…someone else should have a murder. I've had more than my share."

My boyfriend grinned before walking over to the fridge and pulling out the bottle of wine. He refilled my glass—which was nice—but as he went to put the wine away, he stopped dead.

"What is it?" I asked as I followed his gaze to the movie poster for *Spy Diary*.

"Where did you get this?" Rex looked at me curiously.

"I didn't steal it. The manager threw it away." He wouldn't bust me for that, would he?

"Merry." Rex licked his lips. "We found something on the floor of the truck but thought it was nothing."

"What was it?"

"It was this same poster," Rex said. "And now I see it here. In fact, it's the only décor you've ever put up. Can you explain that?"

Now would be the right time to tell him about the movie. Rex knew about my past. But I didn't want Dewey's murder to be on me.

"Merry?"

I sighed heavily. "Sit down. I'd better tell you what I know."

* * *

When I finished, Rex had a dazed look on his face.

"You did *what* with a furnace filter in Mongolia?"

I shook my head. "What I did doesn't matter. It's what's happening *now*. Somebody sold the story of my life to Hollywood. And the Agency will be sending someone to deal with me soon. And now Dewey Barnes—whoever he was—was sent to deal with me also. I'm kind of in trouble."

"What will the CIA do to you?" Rex rubbed his chin.

"I don't know, but it won't be good. Years ago there was this guy who wrote a book about all of his missions—without the Agency's approval. He was never seen again."

Rex rolled his eyes. "Oh, come on! They can't just kill people! That's illegal."

"What? No! He was never seen again because he was sent to work at a science station in Antarctica. They didn't kill him." At least, I think they didn't...

"Why don't you and the girls"—he nodded at the cats—"stay with me for a bit. We can keep an eye on your house and see who shows up. If it looks ugly, I'll send officers over here."

"That's not a bad idea," I mused. "Only Riley and Maria know about you, and they won't tell."

Rex stood up, upsetting the cats. "Come on. I'll get Philby and Martini's things, and you pack a bag."

I rummaged around in my closet and found my suitcase. It took only a few minutes to throw clothes in there. As for the bathroom, I pretty much just scooped everything into the bag and zipped it up. Rex and the kitties were waiting for me by the front door. He had a box of kitty toys, cat food, and a few tins of tuna.

"Let's go," I said as I headed for the garage.

Rex frowned. "Where are you going?"

"To your house," I answered. "I'm just going to take an indirect route in case anyone is watching me."

We piled into the car, and I had Rex duck down. I wasn't going to make it easy for anyone to find me. Maria hadn't called to say they were already here, but if it had been Riley I'd seen and he was in on this, I wasn't taking any chances.

I hit the garage door remote and backed out of the driveway. To anyone watching, they'd just see me in the car. They'd have no idea I had a suitcase or even the cats with me. They'd just think I was running an errand. I took in every vehicle and person as I drove past Rex's house and down the street. Nothing seemed out of place. Maybe they weren't here yet.

After about ten minutes of driving and making sure we weren't followed, I took a very complicated route to the alley behind Rex's house. Pulling into the garage, Rex got out of the car with a cat under each arm. He ran to the back of his house and went in. Five minutes later, I joined him. We left the stuff in the car. We'd bring those in under the cover of darkness.

He closed the curtains and turned to me. "I'm going to run out for takeout. You stay here."

I nodded. I wasn't going anywhere. As soon as he was out the door, I ran upstairs to his bedroom and, with the lights off, surveilled my house. Nothing was happening. Which was good. It was only a matter of time though. I took out my cell and tried Riley again, but it went to voice mail, and I hung up.

I went over the facts in my head. Philby and Martini came in, jumped on the bed, and went to sleep. I'd have to find a way to keep them out of Rex's windows. If the Agency was half the spy company I thought it was, they'd know Rex had no pets and that I did. Seeing Philby in the window would give us away.

The events that led up to this point included a corpse and a movie. Obviously, the movie came first. Probably a year in advance. I grabbed Rex's laptop and googled the movie. A website for something called Black Ops Productions came up. How original. They only listed one movie—*Spy Diary*. Whoever they were, this was their first production.

I clicked on the movie's icon but was sent to a blank site with an apology. This page had already been wiped. I went back to the website, but it was no longer there. The CIA was closing it down.

Heading back to the search page, I found two other listings. One was a review by some movie critic for the *Chicago Tribune*. The other was an interview with the actor who played me. I clicked on that.

A video popped up, and I hit it. The actor was named Max Steele. Really? Max Steele? That's terrible. The actor was smiling at the screen, so I hit play.

"I was so excited to be part of such an amazing movie," the man gushed. "It's an existential look at how our government acts when nobody is watching. The whole movie was a metaphor for political upheaval and how one man can change the course of history."

Please. A metaphor? I know I didn't think it a metaphor when I was being chased by Dobermans in the Netherlands. And one man making a difference? That was annoying. I'm a woman. I did all that. No man did. This guy was trying to make something out of nothing. Well, if nothing had guns and bad guys, that is.

"I'm looking forward to the sequel," Max Steele said happily. "I hear the screenwriter is almost done with the script."

That made me sit up. Now he just needed to say who had written the damn thing so that I could kill him.

"The producer wishes to remain anonymous," Steele said. "They want the focus to be on the art and the philosophy. Their identity might detract from that."

I wasn't sure I could roll my eyes any harder. I tried. It hurt.

"And what's really exciting about this movie," the actor said as he looked carefully around him, "is that it's all true!"

Then the screen went blank. No! Right when I was getting somewhere. The screen then reappeared, but without the video of Max Steele. The guys at Langley were working fast. I quickly clicked on the *Tribune* article. Still there. Great.

Spy Diary *is the most recent, ridiculous load of crap to come out of Hollywood. The producers expect us to believe that this was a true story. That this really happened. Please. I know when I'm being conned.*

Hey! It did really happen!

And if it did really go down like they portrayed—then the spy in this movie was the worst in the history of spying.

Are you kidding me? It all happened! And I received commendations for my work!

Max Steele is the only standout, and even he falls flat as the foolish spy who makes one mistake after another over the course of the film. The writers should be shot and the producers arrested. Don't waste your money on this clunker.

For a moment I toyed with driving straight to Chicago and showing this moron just how true this story was. But then I remembered that I was trying to lay low. Besides, if anyone outside of the Agency did put two and two together to equal me, killing the critic might stand out as a tad unwise.

I waited for the website to disappear, but it didn't. Either Langley liked the review, thinking it was proof that this story was all made up, or they hadn't seen it yet. But they had entire rooms full of analysts who wouldn't have missed something like that, so that theory seemed unlikely.

For ten more minutes I tried to find more intel on the movie, but the CIA had obviously cleared the more damning evidence out. Did they know who the screenwriter was? Would they go after him or her? What about the producers? Were they about to be kidnapped off the streets and taken to a dripping (they were always dripping) and abandoned warehouse to undergo trial by pliers?

I figured Max Steele was pretty safe. He was just an idiot. Too bad that this was probably his last film. Actors probably don't get more work from a film no one has ever seen.

"Merry!" Rex shouted from the back of the house, downstairs.

I made my way down with the laptop under my arm. The food was already plated, and there were two glasses of wine on the table. I set the computer on the sideboard and joined him for the Chinese feast he'd picked up.

While we ate, I filled him in on what I'd discovered.

"Sounds like they're closing in." Rex frowned.

"Well, duh!" I said as I stuffed more sweet-and-sour chicken into my mouth. "What did you think was going on?"

"I just thought you were orchestrating the whole thing so you could move in with me." Rex spoke as if he were asking me to pass the salt.

I stared at him. "You're joking."

He gave me a look I couldn't decipher. "Yes, I'm joking…about the orchestration bit."

"Isn't that the whole thing?"

He shrugged. "It just seems like this is a good time to talk about taking our relationship to the next level."

If you'd dropped a piano on me, I would never have guessed that this was something Rex wanted to discuss.

"Really?"

He nodded. "Yes. Really."

We stared at each other for a moment. Was he saying what I thought he was saying? And what did I think he'd said?

"Um, okay. Let's talk," I finally said.

Philby and Martini trotted into the room. They seemed to be upset that they hadn't been invited to dinner. Rex got up and brought them each a little plate of tuna before sitting down again. That seemed to placate them. For the moment at least.

He looked at me with those stunning eyes. I loved those eyes. I loved everything about him. In fact, we'd only recently started saying the L-word. And why was I calling it the L-word?

"Okay," Rex said before taking a sip of his wine. "Well, where do we want this relationship to go?"

Ugh. He was asking the wrong person. I'd had only one other relationship—and that had been with my former boss, Riley. The man I was hallucinating everywhere. The man who, I'd learned just a few months ago, hadn't actually cheated on me. I'd left him for the wrong reasons. We'd never talked about it since then. As far as relationships went, I wasn't very good at this talking thing.

"I love our weekends together. Renting movies and making dinner. We could maybe do that during the week too?"

Argh! I'm an idiot! This was harder than trigonometry. I was screwing it up, and I knew it.

"Is that all you want from me? A few more dates a week?" Rex studied me.

"Um, yes?" I had a feeling the minute those words left my mouth that they'd been the wrong ones. "I mean, no?"

"What do you want, Merry?"

"What do you want, Rex?" I figured turning the question on him was only fair. Why should I do all the heavy thinking?

"Okay." He nodded. "That's fair. I'd like to see us move to the next level."

The words hung in the air like smog in Beijing. This was a big step.

"You want me to move in with you?" I asked, recalling his words from earlier.

"Yes," he said after a very long pause. Did that mean he wasn't sure?

"I don't know what to say?" I stuffed more food in my mouth.

"Why not?"

"Because I haven't really thought about it." It suddenly seemed like that might've been the wrong answer.

"Why haven't you thought about it?" Rex looked at me intently.

Why haven't I thought about it? We'd been together almost a year now. Did I think we'd just have weekend dates until we died of old age?

"I guess I've just been distracted. There's always some corpse showing up in my yard, or my troop getting into trouble, or my cats…"

He pointed his fork at me. "I think you're ignoring the subject on purpose."

"What? Why? Why would I do that?" I was starting to panic. Because he was right, I had been ignoring the subject.

But why? I loved Rex. I'd told him that. My cats were pretty much his cats. Was I afraid to move on to the next step?

"What exactly," I said as I squirmed in my seat, "is the next step?"

Rex didn't say anything for a few moments, which made me think he didn't know either. That was good. He didn't have a plan in place, and I didn't look like an idiot for not having a plan in place.

Finally, he just gave me a blank look. "You know what? You're right. Forget I said anything."

I swallowed hard. "Okay."

That sounded worse. Either we were putting it off or we were now on the downward slide to breakup land. I didn't want to lose Rex. On the other hand, I wasn't sure what I wanted from our relationship. Was I ready to become a formal couple? And what did that entail exactly? I needed to talk to Kelly. She and Robert had been married forever. Maybe she could interpret what Rex was asking me to do, because it seemed to be more than just moving in together.

How did I end up in this situation? I was just walking along, minding my own business, stepping over all the corpses that seemed to surround me lately, and trying to keep my Scouts from becoming mercenaries. Now my boyfriend wanted more. And worse than that, he wanted me to know what that more was.

We spent the rest of the night in a vague and uneasy silence. The movie was alright, but I couldn't focus. My mind was all over the place wondering what I'd done wrong and how it happened that way.

"Look." Rex turned to me once the movie was over. "I don't want this to be weird. Technically, you're my guest. So I'll make up the guest room for you."

My jaw dropped, but I nodded. We hadn't had many overnight sleepovers. I liked sleeping in my own bed. So using the guest room would be okay. It just left this weirdness between us, and I didn't like that.

As I climbed into bed that night, I cut myself some slack. Tomorrow I'd talk to Kelly. She'd know what to do. And tomorrow I'd start putting this case together. That made me feel a little better.

Now where were Philby and Martini? I heard a pair of mews in the next room and realized they'd abandoned me to sleep with Rex. Great. At least someone was getting a little attention.

CHAPTER SEVEN

Kelly rolled her eyes for like the fifth time during our fifteen minutes together so far—which was like one eye roll for every three minutes—an amount I found a bit excessive. Rex had left for the office in the morning, so I called Kelly and invited her to lunch. The deli on Main Street was empty, so I tried not to be loud. These people didn't need to know my problems.

"I can't believe you!" my best friend finally said. "Rex is a great guy! You are so lucky! Why are you driving him off?"

"I'm not!" I then stalled by stuffing some chips in my mouth so that I didn't have to explain how I wasn't. Because I wasn't entirely sure I knew the answer to that.

"What is the next step?" I asked.

Kelly shrugged. "I think it's pretty clear. He said he wants you to move in with him."

My gut twisted. "I don't know if I want to do that."

"Why not?"

"I love my house. I don't want to give it up. What if it doesn't work out between Rex and me? Then some stranger is living in my house, and I'll have to kill him to get him out."

Kelly ignored me. "It's the only thing I can think of that might be the next step. He didn't ask you to marry him. So what else could it be?"

I wasn't sure I had heard her. "What did you say?"

"He didn't ask you to marry him."

"I don't want to get married. Why can't things just continue on like they have been? What's wrong with that?"

In the back of my mind, I was still worried about the bigger danger of getting kidnapped off the street by CIA agents in a black van. But once again, I was distracting myself from dealing with that.

Kelly pointed a pickle at me. "You need to figure out what Rex means to you. And you need to grow up."

"I am grown up!"

"Right. That's why you cheated at the laser tag game." In spite of her words, she couldn't help but smile.

"The odds were stacked against us one hundred times over. Those boys had it coming."

She nodded. "Yes they did. And what about their leader? So weird!"

I laughed, mostly because I was happy the heat was off of me for now. "I thought maybe he was a robot. No one acts like that."

We talked for a few minutes about other ways we could get ready for the mud run. Which would've been great if we'd had any ideas. Kelly promised she'd look into it. Time was running out.

"What about the dead pizza delivery kid?" Kelly asked. Okay, so she was interested after all.

I brought her up to speed on how the case, which formerly looked bad for Rex, now looked bad for me.

"I can't win!" I grumbled. "I don't know who he is. I don't know how he's connected to the movie or how that's connected to me. All I do know is that someone turned my life story into a bad movie."

"Yeah." Kelly nodded. "That is strange. And the Agency thinks you're in on it?"

I nodded. "To be honest, how could they not? There's stuff in there that only Riley and I should know about, and I didn't even get to see the whole thing!"

"Well." Kelly smiled. "You do talk in your sleep. Maybe some screenwriter has your bedroom bugged."

I glared at her. "I don't talk in my sleep!"

"Yes, you do. The last sleepover—you were talking about some chicken in Chechnya."

The blood drained from my face. "What did I say?"

Kelly shrugged. "No idea. You don't make sense most of the time, and it's worse when you're asleep."

I thought about this. No, I doubted that somehow I'd talked about my entire career while asleep.

"Riley could've told someone," I said at last.

"You don't really believe that!" Kelly protested. She looked shocked. She was definitely Team Riley.

"He's always been my handler, and as far as I know, he's the only other person who knows this stuff."

"You don't really think Riley would sell you out, do you?" She looked mad.

"Hey! You and I have been friends way longer than you've known Riley! How could you take his side?"

"I just don't think he'd do that to you," Kelly said as she went back to eating her sandwich.

"You never can tell." I picked at my chips. My appetite was gone. "Some spies just snap. Others would sell their own mothers for enough money to retire. We're just government employees. We don't make that much."

"Riley did say he was thinking of retiring," Kelly mused. "He thought he'd move here and start a private investigation company."

I shook my head. "When I told you he was thinking of doing that, I should've made you realize that Riley would never retire."

"What people say and what people do is often a mystery to themselves and others."

I threw my hands up in the air. "Whatever. I just don't know if he would sell me out."

Would he? Riley's visited many times over the last year. Was he serious about retiring? Leaving the CIA was kind of a big deal. You had a skill set that wasn't quite transferrable to the non-spying world. I had no choice because the former vice president had outed me. I'd had to leave after that.

"I need to figure this out on my own," I said. "I'll use Rex's computer. I doubt the Company has tapped it."

"How will you do that?" Kelly asked.

I smiled. "Actually, I do have a couple of favors I can call in." Some spies do use their skill set to start their own companies, and that gave me an idea.

"Well, good luck with that." Kelly shoved her empty plate away. And that's when I noticed the dark circles under her eyes.

"What's going on with you?" I asked. "You look terrible."

Kelly agreed. She knew I didn't mean anything bad by it. "I'm exhausted. Robert's been working a lot of overtime, so I'm the only one taking care of Finn most of the time."

"I've never known Robert to do that." I tapped my chin.

Robert worked for the local headquarters of an international farm implement manufacturer. I had no idea what he did, mostly because every time he told me about it my eyes sort of glazed over.

"He got a promotion a few months back. But I think that he's really avoiding taking care of our daughter."

My jaw dropped. "You're joking. Your husband wouldn't do that!"

She shrugged. "It's a lot of work. Plus the hospital can't give me time off because we have two women out on maternity leave. We're strapped."

"Can I help?"

"Not at the hospital. You'd probably kill off half the patients."

"Hey!" I was a little hurt. "I meant babysitting. You could drop Finn off at my…I mean, Rex's place now and then, and you could get a nap in."

"That's not a terrible idea…" Kelly bit her lip. "I could use the sleep. It's either that or a medically induced coma so that I can get some rest."

We went over her schedule for the week and decided I could take Finn the next afternoon for about four hours. This was going to accomplish two things. One, Kelly would see that I am a grown-up. And two, it would distract Rex from talking about moving forward with our relationship. Bonus! We finished eating, and Kelly dropped me back at Rex's through the alley.

Philby met me at the door. Something was up.

"Hey there, girl." I reached down and stroked the top of her head between her ears.

It was her favorite spot, and her eyes usually glazed over. Except for this time. Instead, her eyes were narrowed, and she seemed to be angry. Have you ever had a cat that looks like Hitler glaring at you? It's unnerving to say the least. Martini came racing into the room, eyes bulging. She stopped suddenly then raced back out of the room, her tail about five times thicker than usual. Philby never took her eyes off me.

"I don't have time for this," I explained as I walked past her.

I settled down on the couch with my laptop, facing the window so that I could keep an eye on my house. Maria still hadn't let me know if anyone was on their way to "deal" with me, but I wasn't taking any chances. Philby took up position at the other end of the couch and continued her stare down.

"What?" I asked. She didn't respond.

Ignoring her, I went back to the computer. My cat didn't appear to like this. Within seconds she was sitting on the keyboard, her butt hitting keys that turned the language from English to Swahili, and strange Web pages came up and disappeared again. I lifted the cat from the laptop and set her down beside me.

This didn't seem to deter the feline *führer*. Without taking her eyes off of me, she swatted at my arm. With a sigh I put down the laptop and got up. Philby jumped down from the couch and started trotting toward the downstairs bathroom, looking over her shoulder every few seconds to make sure I was following. I did because this cat wasn't going to leave me alone until she showed me whatever it was.

Once inside the bathroom, she jumped up on the edge of the tub and looked meaningfully from me to what was inside and back to me again.

A dead mouse lay across the drain.

"Did you do that?" I asked Philby, who began strutting around the edge of the tub like a Roman conqueror with tributes.

At this point I wasn't quite sure what I was supposed to do. Philby now added yowling to her swagger, but I couldn't take my eyes off the deceased rodent. Clearly, I was expected to do something.

"Good kitty!" I stroked my cat's head. "Such a brave and vicious killer of mice!"

Philby stopped and gave me a satisfied look. I did something right I guessed. Reaching into the tub, I plucked up the mouse by its tail, and while holding it as far away from my body as I could, moved through the house, went out the back door, and deposited it into the trash can.

I washed my hands for what felt like two hours. It was less of course, but I felt a little like Lady MacBeth trying to get rid of the blood on her hands, if Lady MacBeth had to dispose of dead mice too.

The cats were nowhere to be seen, so I figured it was okay to go back to the laptop. I must've done the right thing because they came nowhere near me. Time to do a little research. I had connections in LA and I had to find them. The good thing about being a spy—someone always owes you a favor. Even if they really don't, most of the time you can convince them that they still do. Spies spend so much time in so many different countries on multiple cases that it's easy to forget to whom you owe what. An hour later I had a couple of phone numbers, and I began to make calls.

"Zeke! It's Finn!" I said as a gruff voice answered. I had to use my spy name, Finnoughla Czrygy, because he probably didn't know I'd changed it to Merry Wrath when I had left the Agency.

"Finn! How are you?" Zeke's big voice was a tonic.

Zeke was a very large man who had been a field agent for ten years when I'd first started at the Agency. By the time I left he'd moved pretty high up in administration. One day, for reasons known only to him, he just up and quit. He moved to LA and became a consultant in the film industry. His specialty was spy movies, but he could pretty much handle everything. That man was a walking encyclopedia when it came to covert activities.

"Um, not so great." I wanted to chat a little, but this seemed like the perfect opening. "Are you on a secure line?"

He laughed. "Of course! I'm not an idiot. What's up?"

"Do you know anything about *Spy Diary*? It just came out..."

"...And was soon shut down. Yeah, I heard about that. But I didn't work on it."

"Do you know who did?"

"Why do you ask?" He didn't sound suspicious. It was a normal question for a person whose life had been clandestine for years.

"Well..." I hesitated a little. Did I really want to drag him into this?

"What's going on?"

After a very heavy sigh I spoke. "There are a few things in that movie that seem to be pages stolen from my career playbook."

There was silence on the other end. It worried me a little because you can take the spy out of the business, but you can't take the business out of the spy. Would he clam up? Tote the Agency line?

"Wow. I didn't know that. And it was such a bad movie."

I wasn't sure if I should be offended by that. I chose not to be. "Yeah. It wasn't great. I saw only about a third before they shut it down."

"And now the CIA thinks you leaked secrets."

I nodded, even though he couldn't see me. "That's right. I'd kind of like to have this tied up before they arrive."

"Okay. I'll see what I can find out. Give me at least twenty-four hours."

"It's a deal." I hung up and felt a little better. Zeke could sniff out a plot like a bloodhound ferreting out the sausages in the deli aisle.

I made a couple of calls after that, but came up empty-handed. Sometimes you get lucky...sometimes you don't. Hopefully Zeke would give me the information I needed.

Now what? Rex was looking into Dewey Barnes' murder, and Zeke was working on intel about *Spy Diary*. What should I do next? I texted Maria but got a message that said she couldn't talk now. That could mean anything. I reminded myself that I shouldn't read too much into that.

It was getting late. Looking at my watch told me it was five thirty. What time would Rex come home for dinner? Was I supposed to get that started? If I moved in here, would he expect me to do that? If so, that might be a deal breaker. Rex ate fairly normal food, while I subsisted on canned ravioli and pizza rolls.

Wow. Thinking about that kind of domesticity came a little too easy. Maybe Kelly was right, and it was time to step up. Rex had a really nice house. It was larger than mine, and he actually had furniture. And nice furniture. I had a couch, a TV, and a crappy coffee table from IKEA that I hadn't put together right. In fact it was only recently that I finally got real drapes to replace the Dora the Explorer bed sheets that had been hanging in my living room. I put them up in my bedroom windows instead. I really liked those sheets.

Rex had a piano and coordinated furniture that matched the floors and drapes. He even had plants. I just wasn't that into permanency. My adulthood had been spent moving from one crappy town in South America to another in Japan. Or Russia. Or the Middle East. A regular routine wasn't my strong suit.

"I guess I'd better make an attempt at dinner," I said to an unimpressed and possibly comatose Martini, who was lying on her back on the table, sound asleep.

The kitchen was well stocked. Rex had pasta, fruits, vegetables, sauces, meat…stuff you could throw together to make dinner. The only area in which he'd failed was in cookies. I'd sold Rex a case of mint cookies. But they were nowhere to be found. I made a mental note to buy a case of Oreos.

I pulled out my cell and opened an app I'd recently discovered. You plugged in the stuff you had in your kitchen, and it gave you a recipe for something you could make. So far I'd managed grilled cheese sandwiches. I always had cheese on hand. Always. I also had a drawer full of takeout menus…just in case.

It took half an hour to plug in everything Rex had in his pantry. Which I thought was weird. How many men kept a fully stocked pantry? Yes, my boyfriend could cook. But it's still strange. My pantry looks like it was very carefully planned by a deranged toddler.

I rejected the first twenty-two recipes because it was like they were written in foreign languages. And I speak Russian, Spanish, Japanese, and Arabic. Words like *whip* and *reduction* and *colander* made me wonder how anyone could understand these things.

I settled on spaghetti because it only had two ingredients—sauce and pasta. Ingredients that I was just organizing when my cell rang. It was Zeke. I answered on the second ring.

"Hey!" I answered. "That was fast!"

"It doesn't take me long. My skills aren't rusty. And there are only a few studios that could've pulled this off."

"What did you find out?" I asked as I pawed through drawers looking for a measuring cup.

"It's Flying Bicycle Productions—a subsidiary of something called Black Ops Productions. And Finn, it's crawling with CIA agents."

"How do you know? Are you there?" I pictured dozens of men in black suits and dark sunglasses poking around a studio lot, trying to seem inconspicuous.

"No. But since you called I've had fifteen different offers for lunch from old contacts who told me they're in town on 'vacation.' You and I know that when agents go on vacation we tend to spend it close to home, not traveling to California."

This was mostly true. We were away from home for such long stretches of time that home seemed like an exotic getaway to us.

"Are they asking you to lunch to pick your brain about *Spy Diary*?"

He laughed. "They can try. The funny thing is, none of them knew that the other fourteen were calling. I've set up lunch with all of them at Spago for tomorrow. I can't wait to see them walk in and realize they weren't the only ones who'd invited me to lunch."

"Put a hidden camera up. I'd love to see the footage."

"Already done. I've been bugging most of the restaurants around here for years. It helps with my 'networking.'"

I thanked him and hung up before he told me that he was blackmailing half of Hollywood. I didn't need any more drama. Dropping everything, I ran for the laptop I'd left in Rex's living room and stopped cold.

Someone was at my house. I slid forward to the window and ducked behind the curtain before glancing out. A man was walking up to my front door, and a strange car was parked in my driveway. Who was it?

The man, who looked to be in his late twenties, knocked on my door. He waited for a few moments before knocking again. Maybe it was just some salesman or something. When I didn't answer the door, because I was across the street, the guy walked over to my front window and peered inside. There was something slightly familiar about him, but I couldn't pin it down. I shoved that thought aside and focused on why this guy was looking inside my house.

Huh. That was a bit creepy. When he saw nothing inside, he walked back to his car. I thought he was leaving, but instead he opened the trunk and pulled something out. In my experience, people almost never do that if they're leaving. Unless there's a body in the trunk…but people rarely open the trunk in public if there's a dead guy in it.

I got a better look at him. I was wrong on the age—he was more likely in his early thirties. And this guy had long, dark hair and was wearing sunglasses with thick, black frames. He was dressed in black pants and a black T-shirt. His overall look screamed *tactical*. And then I saw what he had in his hands. Some sort of long, metal box. Kind of like the tool kit Rex keeps in his garage.

I never called a contractor. Had Rex? He was always saying I needed a real security system. Had he called this guy? And why wouldn't he have told me if he had? It didn't make sense. Alarm bells were going off in my head, and my CIA spy-dey senses tingled. Something was wrong here.

The guy closed the trunk door and started walking the other way. He turned the corner at my garage, and I lost him. This was wrong. All wrong.

Was this guy someone from the Agency? Maria said she'd let me know when they were coming, and she hadn't called. Or maybe it was the guy who'd killed Dewey Barnes, the pizza guy. I wasn't going to wait to find out.

I slipped on my shoes, threw on a sweatshirt and baseball hat, and tucked my gun into my waistband. It was five forty-five. Rex would be home any minute. Should I wait? I could call him, and he'd have a squad car here in minutes.

But then again, what if this guy was booby-trapping my house? It wasn't unheard of, and I'd even gone up against something like that back in the field when a man dressed as a priest had been caught putting a bomb under my doormat. He really shouldn't have done it in broad daylight, nor should he have used a round bomb under a flat mat. Not all spies are smart.

Did I want the cops to walk into a trap? They weren't prepared for that. I couldn't live with myself if anything happened to any of Rex's men. If this guy was laying mines in my backyard, I was the only one who was going to deal with him.

I left the house through the back door and walked nonchalantly across the street—as if I was just out for a walk. An alley ran behind my house, dead-ending before the next house. It was completely overgrown with bushes, so if you didn't know it was there, you'd miss it completely. And it offered a perfect position to spy on my backyard. Of course, this meant anyone else could spy on my backyard too. I'd probably have to rethink that once I figured out what was going on.

I moved carefully through the foliage, trying not to step on a branch and give away my position. In spy movies the agent always runs through the woods with no attention to giving himself away. In real life you moved slowly, watching your feet and your surroundings at the same time. Once, in rural Ukraine, I was tracking a suspected double agent through an insanely dense forest when a large dead squirrel fell out of a tree and landed noisily in an extra crunchy bed of dead leaves. The bad guy had turned around and spotted me before taking off through the trees. I was transferred to Japan the next day. Stupid dead squirrel.

I finally made it to where I could see the back of my house. There was a back door into the garage that was the only entrance. The windows were too high up to get into easily, and I'd nailed all mine shut in my own attempt at home security. I might not be able to cook, but I can nail a window shut like the best of them.

The garage door was open. This guy was probably inside my house. I pulled out my cell and called Rex, but it went straight to voice mail. Should I call 9-1-1? What if this really was just a contractor? Maybe Rex had even told me about it and I'd forgotten. That would make sense. I'd kind of been distracted lately. And if it was true, then, I had a great boyfriend.

I'd always wondered if the guys at the station gave Rex a hard time about me. After all, there'd been a lot of dead bodies around me lately. I didn't want to add to the jokes. If I tackled a contractor called in by Rex, I'd never hear the end of it. On the other hand, if this was a CIA agent coming after me, I'd be better dealing with this alone.

Skirting the backyard so that I couldn't be seen from any of the windows, I got as close to the garage as I could. Finally I crept inside the house as quietly as possible. Standing in the kitchen, I strained to hear any noise.

Nothing.

As far as I knew, contractors made noise. That meant this wasn't a contractor. Which meant one of two things. Either he was here to search and bug my house—which wasn't good. Or he was lying in wait to capture or kill me—also not good.

My house was a ranch house built in the 1950s, so it was all one level except for the basement. From the kitchen, which was in the back of the house, you could go right down the hallway toward the bathroom and two bedrooms or to the left into my living room. But first, I had to see if he'd gone into the basement, which was accessible right by the door to the garage. If he was down there and I checked this floor first, he'd hear me moving around. And that was an advantage I wasn't about to give him.

Fortunately for me, I'd installed my own "system." A small piece of clear tape at the top of the door would let me know if anyone had opened it to go downstairs. The tape was there and intact. That made things easier.

Except for the fact that now I was inside my very small house with a possible killer or the world's quietest contractor. And the only advantages I had were that I knew the layout and he didn't know I was here.

Hitting the camera app on my cell, I crouched down in the kitchen and held it into the hallway. No one was there. I slid to the other side and did the same sweep of the living room.

Again, empty. This gave me another advantage because now I knew he was in one of three rooms at the end of the hallway.

I thought about how to approach this. The bathroom would be the first room on the right. And it not only opened into the hallway, but also into my bedroom. I'd be able to check out two rooms without being trapped in the hall.

Very carefully, I tiptoed toward the bathroom, taking care not to step on the creaky parts of the floor as I went. The bathroom door was open, and I used my cell phone once again to determine if anyone was in there. It was empty. I slipped into the room and very gingerly pushed the door almost closed. But not totally. This guy might remember that the door was open, and if he saw that it was closed, I'd have given myself away.

It bothered me that there'd still been no sound. I didn't even hear any breathing. I knew this guy was inside, but unless he'd gone out the front door, he was in one of the bedrooms. I loosened the grip on my gun.

With a deep breath for resolve, I slid my cell around the corner and into the bedroom. It seemed empty. But then, I had a bed blocking half of my view and a walk-in closet with its door slightly ajar.

Was this guy planning to jump out of the closet and kill me in the middle of the night? That would suck. It was a bit jarring to realize this jerk was either in here or lurking about my guest room. And why was he so quiet? This would be a problem because the floor in my bedroom was pretty creaky. Stepping almost anywhere would give me away.

I thought about the bed and smiled. A few months ago I'd gotten one of those memory-foam mattresses. Maybe if I crawled over that, he wouldn't hear me. But then again, crawling would leave me in a very vulnerable position should he take me by surprise. I pictured myself frozen in mid crawl and how stupid that would look to my attacker.

Looking around me, I spotted a flashlight I kept on the dresser. I could bounce that off the door, which might lead the intruder to come out, guns blazing. But if he wasn't in the closet, that meant he was across the hallway in the guest room, so he'd have time to prepare before I joined him.

If he was in the guest room, he was hunkered down. Either he was working silently, or he knew I was here. I had to either sneak up on him or flush him out. But which one? When this was over, I was going to install hidden cameras in every room. Well, maybe not the bathroom. No one wants hidden cameras in the bathroom.

I still had no idea who this guy was. I kind of wanted to shoot him just for that. So many decisions—each with an equally disturbing outcome. And I had to act fast. So I came up with another idea.

Very carefully, I made my way back through the bathroom and into the hall. I held my breath as I tiptoed to the guest room door and very gently placed my ear against it. Nothing.

I grasped the doorknob and turned it quickly, flinging the door open. I entered the room, gun raised. No one was there. I had cleared the closet and was just walking around the bed when I saw him.

He was definitely dead. The man I'd seen outside stared at me with lifeless eyes, a small hole in the middle of his forehead. I jumped back against the wall and kept my gun trained on the window. A few minutes ago this guy had been alive. Whoever had killed this guy had escaped either through that window or…

Under the bed. If he was under the bed, he could shoot me in the foot at any moment. But if I got up on the mattress, he could shoot up at me through the bed. Five feet away, a rocking chair sat empty. It had belonged to my grandmother. And it was my only chance.

In two long strides I was on the chair, balancing precariously. While I held the gun in my right hand, I used my left to ease open the curtains to the window. It was still nailed shut on the inside. The killer had to be under the bed. How to get him out without him shooting at me?

Oh well. I hated that mattress anyway. I took aim and fired right into the center and waited. Nothing. I fired two more times and waited again. Not a sound. Very carefully I got to my knees on the wobbly chair. Holding on to the bed frame with my left hand, I lowered my right hand to floor level so that the intruder would see my gun. And waited.

Nothing. Not so much as a slight scuff on the floor. Either this guy was dead, or he had nerves of steel. So I fired. Two or three times. The closet door on the other side splintered in protest, but no one made a sound or came out.

I stepped down onto the floor and looked under the bed. There was no one there. The door to the room was still at the exact angle I'd left it ajar when I'd burst in.

With a heavy sigh, I pulled out my cell to call Rex.

"Merry?" My boyfriend was already in the doorway, staring at me, gun drawn. In his back pocket I could hear his cell buzzing from my call. I guessed he wouldn't have to answer it now.

"Guess what." I said. "You have mice."

CHAPTER EIGHT

"Mice? That's why you're shooting up your guest room? Most people just get traps." Rex frowned as he rounded the bed.

He stopped dead when he saw the body on the floor. "Oh" was all he said.

I watched as he knelt down and examined the dead man. "What happened?"

I knew that voice. That was his detective voice. It wasn't the *I'm worried about my girlfriend* voice. I liked that voice.

"I was making dinner," I started.

Rex looked up at me curiously. "You mean you got the spaghetti and sauce out of the cupboard."

I shrugged. "Well, that's the first step in making dinner, isn't it? So, technically, I was making dinner."

"Then what?" he persisted.

"I saw this guy knocking on my front door. He went to his car—which should be in the driveway—retrieved a box, then walked around back."

"And you thought it was a good idea to follow him." It wasn't a question. Rex was making a statement that implied I'd made a questionable decision.

"What if he set up lethal booby traps inside? Or rigged the house to blow? I had to make sure."

He got to his feet and shook his head. In the distance I could hear sirens. Of course he'd called for backup. For the second time in a few days, the police would swarm this neighborhood and remove a body from the premises.

"No," Rex said. "You didn't have to make sure. You should've called me."

I shook my head. "And risk something happening to you? I don't think so."

His eyes narrowed. "I'm a trained police officer. I can handle danger."

I threw up my hands. "So can I! What do you think I did for a living?"

The sirens stopped screaming outside and, in a matter of seconds, two uniformed officers joined us. Rex must've left the front door open. I'd have to talk to him about that.

Detective Boyfriend barked out orders to have forensics search the car out front and look after the body inside. Then he motioned for me to join him, so I followed him to the front yard.

The neighbors were gathering again. At least Elmer was wearing pants, and Ethel was nowhere to be seen. Rex and I had provided a lot of entertainment for these people. This time, however, Kevin and some other policeman were keeping the crowd at bay.

"Go back to my house and wait," Rex grumbled.

"No." I folded my arms over my chest to show him how serious I was. "This is my house. And *my* dead guy. I'm staying."

My boyfriend looked me in the eyes, and I matched the intensity of his gaze. Then he walked away. I guess I'd made him too angry to respond.

Maybe I shouldn't have pushed him on this. Still, I hung around and waited. The forensics team arrived quickly, just before Dr. Soo Jin pulled up and got out. I watched as she commiserated with Rex for a moment. He pointed at me. She smiled and nodded before heading my way.

"Merry," Soo Jin said. "This is awful, isn't it? I'm so sorry this happened. Are the cats okay?"

I was tempted to ask her why she was sorry. I didn't understand why some women were so apologetic. Unless she was behind all of this, I didn't think she should apologize. I let her know that the cats were at Rex's house across the street.

"Rex told me to tell you to stay out of the crime scene." She gave another apologetic face, and I nodded. The coroner went inside the house.

The forensics team pulled something out of the car in my driveway and handed it to Rex. It looked like a manila folder filled with paper. Every single ounce of me was screaming to tackle him and find out what was in the file. But then I remembered something. The window. How did the killer escape through the locked window?

I casually wandered over to it and looked around. No footprints. I glanced at Rex who gave me a sharp look. Well, he couldn't stop me from *thinking* about the investigation now, could he?

I ignored his nonverbal warning and bent down to examine the dirt below the window. Not even the partial imprint of a shoe. I thought about the time frame of the murder. The killer was in the room with the mystery guy. I'd moved in quickly. Somehow the murderer had escaped the room in a matter of seconds. But how had he done it? Perhaps more importantly, why was he in there in the first place? Was that bullet meant for this guy or for me?

I straightened up and looked at the windowsill. It didn't look like anyone had come through it. Reaching up, I tested the window. It didn't budge. My guess was that the shooter hadn't come through here.

A classic locked-room scenario. I loved that sort of thing in books. In reality, it was less than appealing.

There was one other option…suicide. But that option made no sense. This guy was shot square in the middle of his forehead. No one shoots themselves like that. And there wasn't any gun. Oh sure, I hadn't done a thorough search, but in my short time in the room, I should've seen the weapon.

Also, no one shoots themselves in the head and then throws the gun away. Death would be instantaneous. The gun would've dropped to the floor, which meant it would've been in plain sight.

So where was the killer? Could it be that I hadn't done a good job of searching the closet? It wasn't a large one, but I'd been in a hurry. And if so, the guy couldn't have left while I was in there because I'd have seen him, or Rex would've, when he'd tried to leave the room.

I'd fired into the closet. If he'd been in there, he'd be bleeding. But no one was running out of the house shouting about a second body. There wasn't any commotion at all. Which meant the killer had gotten out of the room.

Ugh! My brain hurt. I wandered over to my front door and hovered. I really, *really* wanted to go in. For some reason I obeyed the detective. And resented him for it. Pulling my cell out of my pocket, I called Maria. She didn't answer. I didn't leave a message.

I called Riley next but hit a dead end there too. Was it possible that the dead man in my guest room was from the CIA? That might've made sense. After all, Maria had said they were coming. But she had also promised to let me know when that happened.

Maybe the *killer* was from the Agency? He had seen this guy as a threat and taken him out.

"Tim Pinter." Rex's voice was next to me.

"Who's that?" I asked. "The dead man?"

My boyfriend nodded. "He had ID on him, and that's the name on the car registration and insurance card. Do you know him?"

"No. I've never heard that name." Which was totally true. "Not CIA, then," I mumbled.

Rex asked, "Why not?"

"For one thing," I said, "even if you operate domestically, you don't carry a wallet with your real ID or drive your own car. Never. And secondly, this place would be crawling with men in black suits."

"They're running background checks," Rex said.

"What was in the folder?" I tried to sound nonchalant.

"Tell you what. I'll make a deal with you. If you go home right now..." He nodded toward his house across the street. I followed his gaze and saw that Philby and Martini were plastered to the glass in the front window, standing on their hind legs, front paws on the glass. "I'll talk to you about it when I'm done here."

"You are asking me to leave an investigation at my own house?"

He ignored me. "I'm serious. Head back to my house." He glanced at the window to see both cats pawing furiously at it as if they might be able to get through the glass that way. "And feed the cats."

I considered putting him in a headlock. I considered a sharp, biting response. But in the end I caved and did as he asked. Then I stood in the window with the cats, my hands joining their paws on the glass, and watched until he was done.

"So," Rex said as he walked in the front door half an hour later, "spaghetti?"

I shook my head. "Frozen pizza. In the oven."

The timer went off, and I went to retrieve the pizza. Rex wasn't big on frozen pizza, which is why we always ordered it out. But I'd found one in the freezer that I'd brought over a while ago, before I understood his snobbish ways, and tossed it into the oven.

My boyfriend sighed and mumbled something about going upstairs to change. He was back just in time for me to serve it up.

"Alright," I said, "I did as you asked. Now tell me what you found out."

"We think this is the guy who killed Dewey Barnes. His fingerprints match the ones we'd found on Dewey's truck right at the driver's side window."

"Did you find out what he was doing in my house?"

"No. We didn't find a gun or the toolbox you told me about. Whoever killed him must've taken it."

"So suicide is off the table, then."

"It was never on the table," Rex said. "We just can't figure out how the killer fled the scene. We interviewed the neighbors, but no one noticed anything unusual."

I took a bite of the pizza and chewed while I considered this intel. What was Tim Pinter doing at my house?

"What did you find out when you ran him through the database?"

"Now that's actually interesting." Rex leaned forward. "He's ex-CIA."

"You're joking." I hoped he was. "Retired?" That guy looked way too young to retire. But then here I was, just short of thirty and retired.

"No. Fired. And we couldn't figure out why. That info is classified apparently."

"So Tim killed Dewey and then broke into my house to do…something."

Rex nodded. "Seems that way."

Philby jumped up on the table, and Rex gave her a piece of sausage. Martini had no interest in the sausage because she was busy attacking a piece of cheese that had formed a string. When it finally stuck to every inch of her body, she started munching on it.

"You didn't feed the cats."

I jumped up and poured out two portions of dry food. Both cats gave me a *you've got to be kidding* look that said, *We don't have time for dinner—can't you see we are eating?*

"Dewey was after me and didn't make it. Tim killed Dewey and then took his place. But he didn't make it either."

Rex saw where I was going. "What do they want from you though?"

I shook my head. "No idea. I thought it was something to do with the movie." I told him about Flying Bicycle Productions and how the CIA had invaded Los Angeles.

When I finished, Rex pushed himself back from the table. He'd barely eaten any of the pizza. My guess was that he was going to make a midnight sandwich later.

"Do you know what was in that file—the one we found in Pinter's car?"

I waited somewhat patiently for him to tell me.

"A screenplay. For *Spy Diary*."

I shot out of my chair. "I need to see that! Where is it?"

"I don't have it anymore. In fact I'd just pulled up to the station when two men in suits walked over, flashed credentials, and took it."

My jaw dropped. "You checked them out first. You didn't just hand it over without doing that!"

Rex scowled. "Of course I checked them out. What do you think of me that would make you think that?"

I deflated back into my chair. "Sorry. This whole thing is so bizarre."

And it meant the Agency had sent someone after me without Maria's knowledge. I should've seen that coming. They're not stupid enough to let that leak to one of my best friends.

"I guess I don't need to wait to see if they were going to send someone after me."

Rex was still frowning. "Don't you think they would've made contact with you? What's the point of them 'coming for you,' as Maria said, if they don't actually come for you?"

I put the dishes into the sink and poured myself a healthy glass of wine. "It doesn't make much sense. But then, I have no idea what their investigation of me is about. If you'd asked a few days ago—I'd have said they were trying to catch me handing over classified info to Hollywood. But with all this...I don't know."

I needed to get hold of Maria. Or Riley. This was getting ridiculous. If the Agency was here in my hometown, I wanted to know who and why. And who was killing these lowlifes? Was it the CIA? And what connections did all this have to the movie?

"What did you mean when I found you shooting up your guest room? You said I have mice?"

"Philby killed a mouse in your bathtub," I explained. "Ergo, you have mice."

Rex sighed heavily. "I guess I'd better hit the hardware store for some traps." He got up and grabbed his keys. For a moment he hesitated, as if wondering if he should ask me to go with him. But he didn't. I wasn't sure what to make of that.

I did the dishes, and after he got home, Rex went up to his room to read. He shut the door. I'd really made him mad with that crack about the credentials. Philby yowled outside his door and, when Rex didn't answer, gave me a furious look. Then she started pawing at the door just like she had with the window. I went to bed before finding out if she really could dissolve wood with her paws.

It wouldn't surprise me a bit.

CHAPTER NINE

Rex was gone by the time I got up the next morning. I'd really have to make it up to him. The man was acting weird though, what with talk about taking our relationship to the next level and being overly sensitive about me shooting up my closet. I mean, it's *my* closet.

I got dressed and had a bowl of cereal. Staring out the window, I watched the crime scene tape fluttering on the breeze. I washed my bowl, put on a baseball cap and one of Rex's jackets, and made my way to the back of my house.

The police had been nice enough to lock things up, but they'd also made a mess. Every surface was covered in fingerprint dust. At least that's what I hoped it was. Either that or someone had had a massive cocaine party overnight.

I was careful not to step in the powder or touch anything I shouldn't. They were probably done with the crime scene, but I still had to be careful. Rex was a tinderbox of emotions lately, and I didn't need anything to light the match.

What had Tim Pinter been doing here? He'd had a toolbox. Had he tried to install bugs? For now that would have to wait. I started with the light fixtures in the kitchen, taking them apart and looking them over. I didn't find anything there. Or in the living room. Or the hallway. I went through every drawer and lightbulb socket in the bathroom and both bedrooms but came away empty-handed.

Alright. So he wasn't here to spy on me. What else? The theory was that this guy had killed Dewey Barnes, so my next thought was that maybe he'd come to kill me. But how would he have done that? Most likely he had been planning to lie in wait and shoot or stab me. There's the possibility that he'd have attempted to strangle me, but that didn't seem likely. It took a lot of strength and stamina to strangle someone. And with me being a former spy, he'd know I'd fight back.

No, if he was going to ambush me, he'd shoot. That method was good for maintaining a distance from the victim and not getting as much blood on you. If he'd tried to stab me, he'd have to get close, risking combat. And there'd be blood. Everywhere.

Okay, so if he was after me, he was going to shoot me. But why set up in the guest room? I never went in there. Riley had stayed in that room from time to time, with and without my permission. But I rarely so much as opened that door.

He could be a moron. That might explain why he'd been fired by the CIA. Or he'd been planning to kill me in my sleep. Something like that took patience though. He wouldn't have known I was across the street. He'd have been there a very long time.

I wandered the house for an hour, trying to see if there was anything he'd left behind that would tell me what was going on. It would've been nice to have dropped a digital recorder with a complete monologue of what he'd intended to do, or left behind notes of some sort. Unfortunately, there was nothing.

I examined the guest room. Oh sure, I knew that if there'd been so much as an expended cartridge or anything larger than a piece of lint, Rex would've taken it. I crawled through the closet, shoving aside my winter clothes. I looked under my bed, but other than thwarting an assault from a rabid pack of dust bunnies, I found zip. Zero. Nada. Zilch.

This was driving me crazy. I'd been shut out of Rex's investigation. The CIA agents here in town were avoiding me, and neither Maria nor Riley were accepting or returning my calls. I'd never been so much in the dark in my whole career.

It would have been nice to just wash my hands of the whole matter and let everyone else deal with this…whatever this was. But that was absurd. I needed to know if I was in mortal danger. I needed to know why there was a movie flaunting all the details of my career. And I needed to know exactly what my former employer had in store for me.

I collapsed on my bed and tuned into my surroundings. It was quiet. No cats howling or depositing mice in the bathroom. The TV wasn't on. It was just quiet. I stared at the ceiling and turned this puzzle around in my head over and over, but with the same result each time. I had nothing.

So I got up and looked for anything I'd forgotten to take to Rex's house. I came up with a jacket, a couple of T-shirts and sweaters, and Philby's pills. Poor cat. I'd forgotten to bring her meds, and I'd forgotten to feed her last night. No wonder she'd wanted to sleep with Rex. I couldn't blame her.

I carried the stuff back to Rex's house, grabbed my car keys, and drove off. I couldn't stay here staring at my house and waiting for someone to kill me. Besides, I needed to pick up some junk food for Rex's fridge. No way was I staying there with all that healthy stuff.

I usually went to Clinton's Grocery at the west end of town but today decided to shake things up and go to Marlowe's. Yes, Who's There, Iowa had two grocery stores. And people either went to one or the other. But no one ever went to both.

My parents were Clinton's people. Kelly's family shopped at Marlowe's. It was so strange how I hadn't ever set foot in Marlowe's. But today was the day. I needed a change of place. It might as well come in the form of visiting the "wrong" grocery store.

I pulled into the parking lot and got out. Marlowe's had a very different vibe to it. The setup was like a big store with side-by-side checkout registers. Produce was the first section you entered, and you ended up in the bakery. It was like shopping on a different planet.

My cart was full after I got the hang of the place. I liked it. I'd have to shop there again…I just had to make sure my parents didn't find out. Or Kelly. Marlowe's people liked to gloat when you changed stores.

I was just putting a couple packages of Oreos into my cart when I heard a man's voice on the other side of the aisle. I knew that voice. It was Riley. I'd heard it, in every accent and language, almost every day of my life in the CIA.

Letting go of the cart, I ran down the aisle, skidding across one area where someone had mopped. I turned the corner just in time to see a flash of blond disappear to my left. I ran a few feet to my left, but he wasn't in that aisle. I raced to the next one, but he wasn't there either.

"Miss?" A stock boy had hold of my cart and was shoving it toward me. "You forgot your stuff. We aren't allowed to have unaccompanied carts in the aisles."

I didn't have time for this. "I just need to grab something from the other end of the aisle. Give me a moment, and I'll be back," I shouted as I ran away from him down the other aisle.

"But, ma'am!" he shouted.

I ignored him. As I rounded the end of the aisle, I collided with someone, and we both fell to the floor. I was on top of Riley Andrews. He wasn't going anywhere.

"What the hell?"

I couldn't say much more because Riley threw me off of him and started to get to his feet. Lying on my side, I swept my left leg under him, and he crashed to the floor. This time I flipped him onto his stomach and yanked his arm hard up behind him.

To his credit, he didn't cry out.

"Get off of me, Merry!" He squirmed beneath me.

A crowd had formed. Anxious shoppers looked like they were trying to figure out what to do. I got up and dragged Riley to his feet.

"Are you alright, lady?" a little boy in a Scout uniform asked me. He had to be eight or nine, but he looked like he was going to take Riley out if I answered in the negative. Which was totally adorable.

"Yeah. Fine. Sorry. We were just arguing about the ketchup."

People looked at each other confused.

"I'm a loyal Heinz fan. Go, Heinz!" I cheered as I dragged Riley around the corner to where the stock boy was waiting with my cart.

"Thanks," I said to the boy. He shook his head and walked away.

No one saw as I slammed Riley up against the canned goods. "You are in big trouble."

"Merry, I…" he started.

I interrupted, pulling him down the aisle with one arm and pushing my cart with the other. "You are coming with me now. You will not struggle or escape. In fact—" I eyed the cart. "You are paying for my groceries."

Riley acted like nothing was wrong as he paid for six packages of cookies, four bottles of wine, two cans of squeezy cheese, two boxes of cheddar crackers, a box of cereal that largely consisted of sugar, and several boxes of Twinkies. I even made him load the car.

I was furious and relieved at the same time. On the one hand, Riley really was here. I'd seen him, and he'd avoided me. And he hadn't taken my calls. On the other hand, Riley was here. Someone connected with the CIA. He could help me by handling all this unwanted Agency attention.

"I wanted to tell you," Riley said once we were buckled into our seats.

"Why didn't you? You've been here all this time, and you never let me know. In fact you wanted me to think I was crazy and hallucinating."

He shook his head. And that's when I noticed his hair was short. Really short. Riley had always rocked a surfer vibe with thick, wavy blond hair just a bit longer than was allowed.

"You cut your hair!" I accused.

"I know this looks bad," he said as he ran his hand through what was left, "but I can explain."

I folded my arms over my chest. "Well?"

Riley's eyes darted around the parking lot. "Not here. Somewhere else."

"Do you honestly think they bugged Marlowe's? Impossible! I've never shopped here before today, so the joke is on them!"

"I'm more worried about being watched than overheard."

I thought about this for a moment. We couldn't go to my house because I'd already done that and didn't want to run the risk of Rex finding out. And we couldn't go to Rex's house because that seemed…inappropriate somehow.

"Okay," I growled as I slid the key into the ignition. "I'll take us somewhere private. But you are going to spill it when we get there."

"Agreed." Riley seemed relaxed, but he scanned our surroundings as I drove across town to a playground.

"Here?" Riley asked. "Why here?"

"Because no one would ever think of looking for either of us here." I shut off the engine and locked the doors. Just in case.

"So." I turned toward him. "What do you have to tell me? And remember, I have a mean right cross."

Would I have hit him? Probably not. But I was really mad. His excuse had better be good.

Riley moved to run his hands through his hair—a gesture I'd seen at least a million times. Unfortunately his hair was too short to do so now, so he stopped in mid-gesture and turned to look at me.

To be completely honest, he didn't look half bad with shorter hair. It somehow made his eyes look even larger.

"Okay," he said with a little shake of his head, "I'll tell you what's going on. I'm not here at the behest of the Agency."

"Oh," I said quietly. "So you're here because…why, exactly?"

Riley frowned, and I realized he was starting to develop frown lines between his brows. Wow. That was telling. This guy took better care of his skin than I did. Something's been eating away at him.

"Well…" He started fiddling with his shirt. This was a red flag also as Riley never fiddled with anything. The man oozed confidence. "I think I might be the cause of the movie leak."

You could've knocked me over with a butterfly's wing. Riley was the reason for the movie? Now I really wanted to hit him.

"This is *your* fault? You put my whole life up there on the big screen? Are you nuts?"

He held up his hands defensively, but I wasn't going to deck him…yet.

"It's maybe possible that some of my notes have disappeared."

"You're saying that a few notes are missing?" I crushed the steering wheel between my fingers. "Riley! That was my whole career in that movie! I think 'some of your notes' doesn't cut it!"

"I know." He chewed on his lip—another completely bizarre thing for him to do. "I'm not really sure how it happened. I thought everything was locked up."

"What? Did you keep your notes under your pillow? And why did you even have those notes? All of these cases are still classified!"

"Um…well…that's a very good question…" He stared off at the playground.

"And the answer is?"

He shrugged. He actually shrugged. My life and career were falling apart in an episode that one critic called "the most unrealistic movie ever," and he shrugged.

"Why hide from me?"

Riley ran his hands through his now very short hair. "I wanted to see if you were behind this."

I put the car in gear and backed out of the parking lot.

"Where are we going?" my former handler asked.

"To Rex's house. I have a lot of questions, and I'm sure the police do too." I pulled out onto the street. "But I think the Agency is watching the police, so we're going to the one place I think we might be safe."

To his credit, Riley didn't argue. He just sat there in the passenger seat, eyes on the road, as I drove. We pulled into the alley behind Rex's house minutes later, and I made him bring in the groceries.

Philby and Martini came running and, when they saw Riley, rubbed against his leg, moaning loudly. For the first time, I saw him smile as he bent down and scooped up the cats. Either he'd missed them, or he figured I wouldn't punch him if he was holding twenty pounds of adorable.

He was right. I led him into the living room and pointed at the couch. He sat. Then I sat in the chair facing him. I was pretty pissed off. There was no way I was going to give him a chance to use his charms on me.

That tactic had worked before. I wasn't going to give in to them this time.

"Talk," I said.

Riley gave a loud sigh, and the cats looked up at him expectantly. He stroked their little heads until both cats were asleep on either side of him.

"Now," I insisted.

"I'd made a few notes about our experiences in the field."

"Why would you do that?" I asked. "You know we can't do anything with that intel. It's classified for, like, ever."

"I'd kind of thought that maybe someday I'd write a book," he muttered.

CHAPTER TEN

"You *what?*"

My cell buzzed. I was about to turn it off, in light of the huge disagreement Riley and I were about to have, when I saw the text message: *Leaving now to drop Finn off.*

Oh crap. I forgot I was supposed to babysit Finn today. I couldn't back out. Kelly really needed a break.

"You have to go." I got up and pulled Riley off the sofa. Philby and Martini woke up and complained loudly. "We will resume this later. But I'm babysitting Finn in a few minutes, and I don't want our goddaughter to see us fighting."

"Fine." Riley sniffed. "I'll go to your house."

I was about to protest, but then realizing that he'd have to sleep on a mattress full of bullet holes seemed strangely satisfying, so I handed him a key.

"When I'm done"—I glowered at him—"you're coming back here and explaining this to me."

Riley said nothing. He just walked out the front door of Rex's house and into the front door of mine. I heard the door slam just as Kelly pulled up.

I ran outside, shoving all of my anger aside and pasting on a smile. Kelly got out and handed me my sleeping namesake, still in her carrier. All of my fury melted away, and my heart was filled with warm, fuzzy thoughts. Finn was so adorable! I'd show her and her mother that I could handle responsibility. Riley could stew across the street. He could wait. I needed a few hours with this baby.

"Hold on." Kelly walked around to the trunk. "I've got the rest of the stuff."

Rest of the stuff? Oh. She was talking about bottles and that kind of thing. That would be easy too. I'd googled formula and found out the ratio to mix is on the container. In fact I was feeling pretty proud of myself. Whatever else she had in the car, I could handle it.

I was wrong.

Kelly pulled out a pink bag that looked like something a soldier would take with him on a two-year international assignment. I wasn't even sure I could lift it. Okay, I could handle that. She was just being thorough. I probably wouldn't need it much.

"Here's her special chair." Kelly grunted as she lifted something that looked like fabric flung across two bent wires. "I usually feed her in this. Just don't set the vibration too high or she'll spit up."

Vibration?

A long, large basket came next. It was white wicker and had a little mattress inside.

"She sleeps in this." Kelly set it on the sidewalk next to the other stuff.

"She can't just sleep in her car seat thingy?" I asked.

"Is that a baby?" I hadn't noticed that Ethel, the old deaf lady next door, had joined us.

"She's sleeping!" I hissed.

"Ethel?" Elmer called from inside the house. "Someone stole my pants!" He stepped out on the stoop wearing boxers and a T-shirt.

In spite of the fact she was sleeping, I covered Finn's little eyes, thus demonstrating to Kelly that I was responsible.

"It's a baby!" Ethel clapped her hands together in glee.

"I'll come out..." Elmer started down the steps toward us.

I scooped up the giant pink bag in one hand and, with the baby in the other, fled into the house. I set the carrier down and did the fastest run ever to the sidewalk to get the chair and basket. Kelly had already driven away. Apparently, she didn't want to see Elmer and his missing pants.

By the time I got back inside, Philby and Martini were sitting next to the carrier staring at Finn, who was fortunately still asleep. These three had been acquainted for some time, but the cats looked confused that the baby was on their turf.

"Let her be, guys," I whispered as I gently lifted the carrier and put it on the dining room table.

Philby jumped up beside the baby while Martini found a sunny spot on the floor and passed out.

"Kelly won't be back for a few hours," I told the cat for some reason. "We need to take good care of Finn, okay?"

I wasn't sure why I was asking my cat to do this. But hey, she was a mom. Maybe she'd had some experience in this area. Not that I needed any help. The baby was snoozing peacefully and would probably stay that way until Kelly returned. Easy.

Philby walked over to the giant pink bag and sniffed gingerly. Which peaked my curiosity. What was in there that was so important that Finn couldn't be without it for even two hours?

After a glance at the baby to make sure she was still asleep, I sat down on the floor next to Philby and unzipped the bag. It was packed so tightly that it burst open. Dozens of tiny diapers, two huge boxes of wet wipes, one large canister of formula, a gallon of distilled nursery water, and ten baby bottles popped out of the opening.

Take a deep breath, Wrath. You'll be fine.

I picked up one of the diapers. At least these were disposable. I don't know what I'd do if they were cloth. I opened it up and saw that one side had little tape thingies and there was elastic around the leg holes. But how did it go on the baby? With the tape in front or back? I gave Philby a look.

She didn't go anywhere. In fact she just lay there on her back as I proceeded to put the diaper on her. Hmmm…the tail would be a problem. Jumping to my feet, I ran into the kitchen and returned with scissors. I cut a hole on both sides that I thought would be generous enough and reapplied the diaper to my cat.

Philby made no complaint. Either she understood that with her help a major crisis would be narrowly avoided, or she was plotting my murder in the middle of the night. It only took a few tries to realize that the diaper worked best with the tabs in the back. Philby stood, and after arching her back, strutted around the house wearing the diaper—her tail flicking wildly back and forth.

The baby began to cry, striking terror into my heart, and I ran over to check on her. Finn saw me and smiled. Well, that was good. Maybe she just wanted to be held. I lifted her from the car seat and discovered that her diaper had tripled in weight and smelled like a dead animal. No problem! I knew just what to do!

I grabbed a towel from the bathroom and laid the baby on it. With a stack of diapers and both boxes of wipes, I carefully pulled the tapes off and slid the diaper out from under her.

Oh. My. God.

The contents of the diaper was enough to make me grab my cell to call for help. I hung up halfway through tapping out the number. Kelly was taking a nap. She did not need me interrupting to tell her I think her baby had expelled the equivalent of a New York City sewer. It could be that this was normal—and if it was, I was never ever having a baby.

I wrapped the diaper up and re-taped it, feeling pretty proud of myself that I'd managed to get none of that toxic sludge on anything else. Then I opened the box of wipes and pulled about forty out.

They were cold. How did I know that? From the look of shock that crossed Finn's face when I began cleaning her up. I tried to do it quickly, but the wipes were thin and not very absorbent. It took half the box before I felt like my goddaughter was clean enough to diaper. The pile of wipes was about three feet tall. I wanted to throw them out, but I couldn't leave Finn.

Philby walked past, still wearing her diaper, her tail still switching violently. She hadn't taken it off. That seemed a little weird, but then cats are strange.

Finn smiled at me and began kicking her legs furiously. It stopped me in my tracks. Was she having a seizure? She kicked her legs in a bicycle-like pattern, her fists opening and closing, and now her face was the picture of concentration. Was she trying to run? Where would she go? I know she's old enough to sit up on her own, but was she able to walk? At least she wasn't upright.

I slid the diaper beneath her little bottom and taped it together. The seizure stopped. Clearly I'd just saved the day from something. Now where should I put her? The basket thing was out of the question because she wasn't asleep. And it seemed cruel to put her back in the car seat. That left me with the weird chair Kelly had mentioned earlier.

I put the contraption on the table. It looked like a baby slingshot. That didn't seem right, catapulting babies. But what did I know? I noticed a strap in front that appeared to connect to the chair on each side, with holes for the legs, and I quickly strapped her in. After congratulating myself for figuring that out, I took the dirty diaper and wipes to the kitchen, where they filled the trash can.

Finn began running again, and the chair started to bounce up and down. That was cool. I'd kind of like a chair like that. No matter how hard she kicked her legs, the chair absorbed the movement, and she seemed to like that. Maybe I should feed her while she's trapped. Wouldn't Kelly be impressed that I'd changed her diaper and fed her? That would be a total win-win.

There were ten jars of baby food in the bag. Seriously, how long was Kelly planning to be gone? I unloaded them, placing the jars side by side on the table for closer inspection. There were carrots, peas, squash, and many more vegetables and fruits—all looking equally disgusting. Pears. I'd go with pears. Sure I wanted props for feeding Finn, but there was no way I was giving her something icky. I was going to be the fun godmother who only dished out the good stuff, so pears it would be.

The jar opened easily, which was nice. And Kelly had packed a long, tiny spoon coated with rubber. When Finn saw it, she started licking her lips and kicking harder. Oh yeah, I'm a natural. I can already read her and know what she needs. Kelly would be all *Merry! You're my savior!* And *You are the best godmother in the universe!*

I dipped the spoon into the goopy liquid, bringing up a very healthy portion. Finn opened her mouth and clamped down on the spoon. But as I pulled it away, she spit the food back out, and it ran in blobs down her chin.

I grabbed the wet wipes and used the other half of the box to clean her up, congratulating myself on not feeding her the obviously staining prunes or carrots. But how did I keep her from doing this again? A moment of inspiration hit, and I snatched a dish towel from the kitchen, gently tucking it under Finn's chin.

Philby jumped up onto the table and trotted over, the diaper crinkling as she sat down. She would hopefully sniff the spoon and pull away. What? Did she think I'd feed the baby tuna? Clearly Philby didn't know anything about babies.

Not like me. I was quickly turning into an expert on babies. And that was without training.

We tried a smaller spoonful, and Finn didn't spit it out. This was good because I was wondering if I could wrap her in a towel, shove the food down her throat, hold her mouth closed, and blow on her face like I had to when medicating my cat.

Halfway through the jar, Finn seemed less enthusiastic. She wanted to grab Philby who for some reason didn't have a problem with that. My cat just sat there while a baby tore out handfuls of fur. I was so impressed that I decided the cat would get a whole tin of tuna tonight.

That's when I noticed the buttons on the side of the chair. *On* and *Off* they said, daring me to touch them. What did they do? Kelly said something about it…but I couldn't remember. So should I turn it on? It couldn't be that bad if it was on a baby chair, right?

I switched the on button, and the chair began to vibrate. Nice. Now I really wanted a chair like that. Maybe one big enough for me and Rex. Finn's chubby cheeks were jiggling, and we both smiled. This was a good thing! Finn liked it! So, of course, I decided to turn it up to the next level. I mean, if she liked this, she'd love the next level, right?

I hit the button again, and this time the chair vibrated so hard that it started to move across the table. Well, that was not good. I had just pulled the chair from rocketing off the edge of the table when I noticed that Finn's eyes were open wide like she wanted to tell me something. That was when it happened.

She barfed. Not just on herself and the towel…but on the chair. On me. On the table. Somehow Philby escaped the mess, but I was covered in regurgitated pears. I switched the chair off and remembered what Kelly had said. Oh. Right.

I mopped the baby up using half of the other box of wipes (it now made sense that my best friend had packed so much) and stripped off my T-shirt. My bra was a little wet, but it wasn't vomit stained, so I didn't worry about it. I lowered the chair to the floor, and Martini bounced over, wondering what she'd missed. Upon seeing Philby's diaper she dragged one out of the open bag and brought it to me.

I should've put on another shirt, but Martini was pretty insistent. So once again I got out the scissors, only making a hole on one side this time, and diapered the kitten. Martini strutted around like she was the living end while I threw another huge stack of wipes into an overflowing kitchen garbage can.

When I came back into the living room, something seemed off, but I couldn't put my finger on it. Finn was cooing at the cats. The cats were sitting there…wait…what's that in Philby's mouth?

A long, skinny piece of gray yarn dangled from her mouth. Which was weird because as far as I knew, Rex hadn't taken up macramé. Was the piece of yarn…moving?

Philby lowered her head to the floor and spit out a mouse that was running before his four feet hit the floor. The two cats started chasing the mouse, which was dodging his feline Stormtroopers by running in circles around the baby chair. I ran over and tried to swat at the mouse, but he'd decided it was safer being around me than the cats.

"Go! Get! Scat!" I shouted as I waved my arms at the rodent.

Philby and Martini split up, each stalking their prey from a different direction. They no longer resembled the snuggly cats I knew and looked more like the hunting velociraptors from *Jurassic Park*…if those velociraptors had diapers on, that is.

Finn, determined to get in on the fun, began to squeal loudly, kicking her legs and waving her arms. She knew something was up and decided she wanted in on this action. The mouse was on its back legs, trying to decide which way to go as Philby and Martini closed in.

This was not good. I needed to get the mouse out of here before Kelly came back. If she knew I'd allowed a mouse around the baby, it wouldn't matter how many diapers I'd changed or vegetables I'd fed her—I'd never be forgiven.

Unfortunately, the mouse wasn't interested in scoring brownie points for me. He'd figured out an escape route by jumping up onto the baby's chair and racing toward her head. Philby and Martini decided this was a great idea and also jumped onto the chair and the baby. Finn giggled and squirmed as the mouse stopped right above her head. It looked like she was being swarmed.

Without thinking, I shoved the cats off the chair and, reaching behind the baby, pulled the head of the chair back as far as I could before releasing it. The mouse soared through the air, where Philby jumped up and caught it. It was pretty epic. At least no one was there to see it.

"What am I looking at?" Riley's voice came from behind me.

Okay, so this looked bad. He'd walked in to see me shirtless, launching a mouse from Finn's head while my cat snatched it out of the air.

"Why are the cats wearing diapers?" Riley asked as he walked over and unsnapped Finn from her seat, lifting her into his arms. "Why are you letting them put mice on my goddaughter? And why aren't you wearing a shirt?"

The open leer on his face told me that he didn't mind that last part at all.

A million explanations went through my mind, from the truth to a story where the cats put on the diapers and Finn picked up the mouse.

"Why are you here?" I asked.

"I saw you running around like a maniac in a bra," Riley said as he snuggled Finn. "I could see it all from your picture window. I thought something was wrong, and I knew the baby was here."

That seemed legit. I made a mental note to close the front drapes next time. If there'd even be a next time.

"Hold Finn. I'm going to find a shirt." I ran for the stairs.

"You can stay like that…if you want to." Riley grinned.

There was no way I was going to want Rex walking in to find me in a state of undress with Riley, so I ignored his comment and ran upstairs. Reappearing in minutes, wearing a new, vomit-free T-shirt, I walked over to Philby, who once again had a mouse tail dangling from her lips.

"Give me the mouse." I held out my hand.

Not that I actually expected her to do that. And she didn't. Philby kept the mouse and trotted into the bathroom. I followed to find her toss the animal into the tub and climb in with it. The mouse was trapped. Closing the door behind me, I joined Finn and Riley in the living room.

"How did you get in?" I asked.

"The door was unlocked."

"I'm sure I locked it." At least that was what I'd tell Kelly. Strike one against me, except for the mouse-on-the-baby thing.

Riley sat down on the couch with the baby. "Tell you what—I won't tell Kelly about the mouse and the unlocked door if you'll hear me out."

I narrowed my eyes. "I don't want to fight in front of the baby."

I wasn't sure if there was a way for Finn to tell Kelly what happened here. My guess was that, unless she was beyond her years when it came to pantomime, Kelly would never know.

"Fine. I'm going to hold you to that."

Riley nodded. "It's important that you understand what happened."

"You said you wrote about things that happened in the field." I snatched Finn from his arms and sat on a chair.

Riley had the good grace to look embarrassed. "I know it was stupid. But you have to admit—we've had some pretty crazy stuff happen in the field. I figured someday it would make a great book."

"We? The movie didn't have *you* in it. It only had some nitwit playing me! And why the hell was I a guy anyway?"

"You can't blame me for that! I had you as a woman in my manuscript."

I stared at him. "So in the last five minutes it went from being a few notes to a full manuscript. If you keep lying to me, I'm going out to the garage to get Rex's blowtorch."

Riley rolled his eyes. "Now you're just overreacting."

I covered Finn's ears before I blew up. "*Overreacting??* Are you joking? I just saw my whole career played out on the big screen. The CIA is coming to get me...whatever that means...and we have two dead bodies because of your stupid little book!"

"Hey!" he said a bit defensively. "It's not stupid! It's a good book! I've put a lot of time into that, and it was totally ready for pitching."

"When? In thirty years when all of those cases become declassified?" Wait...did he just say it was polished and done?

I looked down and saw that Finn had fallen asleep. Very quietly I carried her into the dining room and put her into the basket thing, moving it to the doorway so that I could see her, but hopefully she wouldn't be able to hear us.

"I figured I might be able to approach the deputy director to get a pass..." Riley scowled. "Did you say two dead bodies?"

I threw my hands into the air. There was no reasoning with him. At this point I resorted to chewing him out.

"Most of the book would have to be redacted! You know this! You've seen what's happened to agents who've written books before!"

My first year out of the Farm (the training location for agents), a guy I didn't know had tried to sell his book about his experiences in the UK. The UK! And his stuff was boring! I guess he'd rescued one of the queen's corgis once or something. And he wasn't just shut down—he was transferred to Greenland for twenty years. And, as we all know, nothing ever happens in Greenland. As far as I knew, he was still there.

Another time, two secretaries wrote a novel together about a fictional field operative in Chile. They made up the whole book. Not one word was true. And they got sent to the mail room. Permanently. Greenland was a better alternative to the mail room at Langley. It was dingy, and they had bats.

"Two dead bodies, Wrath." Riley was no longer struggling. His calm, composed manner was back. "Explain."

I could've argued with him, but what was the point? The only way to get any real answers was to tell him what had happened. So I told him about Dewey the Pizza Guy and Tim Pinter. Riley listened quietly, patiently taking it all in.

"So you didn't have anything to do with those murders?" I asked.

He shook his head. "No. Why?"

"I had kind of hoped it was you who killed Pinter."

"You just said you fired your weapon through the guest room bed and closet! You thought you were shooting me?"

"No. Not at the time. But later I thought you might have been behind it."

His eyes narrowed. "I don't kill in cold blood, Wrath. And not just for a movie."

"Maybe you were worried Pinter was booby-trapping my house. He was ex-CIA."

The two of us considered this quietly.

"You didn't know him, did you?" I asked.

"Never heard of him. But that doesn't mean anything. I don't know everyone."

That was true. The CIA didn't exactly have an annual yearbook or interoffice newsletter. There were a lot of spies I didn't know even existed.

"I can ask Maria…" I started.

Riley cut me off. "I don't think you should do that. We don't know how far up this goes."

My jaw dropped. "You're joking. I totally trust Maria. It's you I'm not so sure of."

This seemed to anger Riley, and he said nothing in reply. Had it hurt when I'd said that? Trust was so important out in the field. You had to trust the people you worked with because there was no one else.

"You should trust me, Merry," he said quietly.

"Why should I trust someone who's been in town, shadowing me for days, without letting me know?"

"I couldn't tell you anything until I knew what was going on."

"Really? Or were you hoping you could figure out who stole your damn book and leave town before I even knew you'd been here?"

"That's not fair," he said.

"What's not fair"—I picked up the conversation—"is you not answering my calls. Is you writing a secret book about *my* exploits that you hoped to make money on—and we're going to get back to that, by the way. You've been hiding from me."

Riley took a deep breath. "I didn't kill your pizza man or the ex-agent in your guest room. I swear it. I have no idea who they are."

I tried a different track. "Does the CIA know you're here?"

"Not exactly…"

"Not exactly? Could you be more specific?"

"They think I'm on vacation in the French Riviera."

"Should I make french fries tonight so that you can feel you're really there?" I sniped.

Riley didn't answer.

"So you've gone rogue."

Going rogue wasn't like you see in the movies or on TV. Going rogue was a career-ending decision with the possibility of jail time. Significant jail time.

"I honestly thought I could take care of this without you knowing."

"It's kind of hard to do that when the CIA thinks I'm the leak. They're swarming Hollywood as we speak. Zeke says fourteen agents at least."

He frowned. "Zeke? You talked to Zeke?"

I stared at him as if he'd grown a unicorn horn out the middle of his forehead.

"Well, duh. He's my only contact there. I was hoping he'd know who was behind this." I thought about what he'd said minutes ago.

"Hey! You were hoping to leave town before I knew you were here! Did you think I'd just get blamed for your screw-up and you could head back to the Riviera and let me take the fall?"

"I wasn't hoping for that. I was hoping they'd see that you weren't involved and leave you alone."

"After a full investigation!" It didn't matter that I'd left the Agency a couple of years ago. I'd still be under suspicion on a possible actionable offence.

"I hoped it wouldn't go that far," he responded.

I sighed. "You were pinning your getaway on a lot of iffy hopes."

"So what now?" he asked.

"What do you mean?" I said darkly. "You are going to explain to Langley that you screwed up. That your book fell into the wrong hands. That I had nothing to do with all of this."

"I'm not sure that's a good idea." Riley steepled his fingers.

"For you, maybe. But for me, totally. You do realize that someone invaded my home to do who knows what. Your actions could've gotten me killed."

How could I make him see that this was a huge mess? Riley had never done anything like this before. Who was this idiot in Rex's living room? Not my once loyal partner. This Riley was dangerous. This Riley wanted me to take the fall for his own stupidity.

"Okay. Fine," he said.

"What do you mean by that?" I asked.

"I'll stay here and help you find out what's going on."

My sarcasm went into overdrive. "Oh, thank you. That would be such a big help. What would I ever do without you…besides being blamed for something I didn't do, I mean?"

"What's going on?" Rex asked from the doorway to the kitchen.

"Why is your cat wearing a diaper?" Kelly asked from the front door. She checked out the bassinet and seemed relieved to find the baby in it.

I really had to do something about my best friend thinking I was a bad babysitter.

"Riley has finally decided to come out of hiding and join us," I said. "He's going to use all of his resources to find out what's going on. Isn't that right?" I turned to Riley.

He grimaced. "Do I have a choice?"

I shook my head. "No. You do not."

Rex cleared his throat. "Well, I brought dinner from the new Italian place. I'm sure there's enough for four. I think we should sit down and have a little chat."

Kelly waved us off. "I should get home. Thanks for watching her, Merry. I didn't realize you'd have Riley helping you."

Through clenched teeth I said, "He just got here. He didn't help me. I did it all by myself." I explained the changing of the diaper and the feeding of the pears.

Kelly looked unimpressed. Rex and Riley helped her pile everything into the car, and we watched as she drove away.

Oh well, at least we didn't have to split dinner four ways now. I could fill Kelly in later on what an amazing babysitter I was. We walked back into the house and heard a fierce flurry of cat paws coming from the bathroom. Rex opened the door, and a proud, diapered cat strutted out.

"Oh, yeah, and there's a mouse in your tub," I said.

Rex took the now dead mouse out back while Riley and I got the food out, and I made my former boss swear not to tell Rex what had happened here either.

As we ate, Rex filled Riley in on the stuff I'd just told him. He just went into more detail than I had. At least Riley listened. I would've spoken up a few times, but the garlic bread and ravioli were so good that my mouth was full the whole time. I needed to know more about this new Italian restaurant. I wonder if they'd set up a regular delivery.

"The screenplay? You found a copy of the screenplay?" Riley asked. "I need to see that."

Rex looked at me questioningly.

"He wrote the book the script was based on," I muttered as I snatched up another piece of bread.

Rex turned slowly to Riley. "You wrote the book? What is she talking about?"

Riley stalled. My guess was that he didn't want Rex to think the same things I'd thought—that Riley had written a book about my life and was hoping to exploit it for his own financial gain. I waited to see what he'd say.

"I wrote a book. About our time together in the field. It was all work stuff. And it was somehow stolen and made into this movie."

I gave Rex a sort of I-don't-know-what-to-think-about-that look that hopefully told him I wasn't involved.

"Can I see the screenplay?" Riley asked with the confidence of a man who didn't have a care in the world. It was a dangerous game, considering that Rex might just take offense to the idea that my former boyfriend was using me to become a best-selling author.

"I suppose…" Rex answered. "They confiscated it but just shoved it into a desk drawer. I'll snag it and bring it home tonight. But you'll look at it here. It won't leave my house. And I'm taking it back tomorrow morning."

What? Rex was going to help Riley? Riley didn't deserve that.

Riley nodded. "Thanks."

Rex said, "No problem."

What was happening here? Was I the only one who thought I'd been screwed? And not in the good way?

"But after dinner I want you to head over to Merry's house. She's going to walk you through what happened. I'm sure she's already ignored the caution tape." He gave me a look.

I was going to deny it, but he was right.

"She's in danger, and I want you to keep her safe."

Okay, that was nice.

"But my station is crawling with agents that I'd like out of my hair. I'm giving you three days. If you can't find out what's going on, I'm turning you in to your superiors."

Ooh! Way to drop the hammer! I liked it!

Riley thought about this for a moment while Rex and I continued to eat. It was taking a little too long. I was about to brain Riley with a chair when he finally spoke up.

"Of course. It's the least I can do."

The men shook hands, and Rex headed back to work. It was late, but he'd explained that with the CIA in town there was a considerable amount of paperwork that had to be done.

Riley put the leftovers away and washed the dishes. I just stood and watched. I was still pretty angry with him. None of this selfishness was like Riley. He'd never sold me out before. Or maybe he'd just never had the opportunity or need to do so in the past.

Had he always been like this? How could I have missed it? Up until an hour ago, I'd trusted my former handler with my life. Now I wasn't so sure. It made me wonder if I was a bad spy. That I'd missed all the telltale signs over the years. I couldn't remember him following me around with a notebook and pen or using a digital recorder when I reported in. From what I'd seen so far, he must've been taking notes because my memory wasn't that thorough.

It could be that Riley was behaving like this for the first time. That he'd come up with the idea of writing the book, completely overlooking the fact that it was a terrible idea. Forgetting the fact that I'd be the first person the CIA looked at.

Part of me wanted to grab the cats and run away until this was sorted. I figured I could take a vacation myself. Let Riley handle it all while my kitties and I sunned ourselves on an obscure, hidden-away beach somewhere. I wondered if cats could get sunburned.

The other part of me though, the one that was far more logical, wanted to keep an eye on Riley. Stick to him like glue. Make sure he followed through with Rex's directive. Give him a chance to prove he wasn't a world-class jerk. And if he didn't shoulder the weight, I'd turn him in.

I'd have to decide soon. The dishes were done, and Riley was standing there, staring at me. I guess I'd been in la-la land a little too long.

I pulled my keys out of my back pocket. "Let's get this over with," I said as I pushed him out the back door.

* * *

"You shot my bed?" Riley stared at the guest room mattress, stunned.

"Your bed? This was never your bed." Granted, Riley had the bad habit of dropping in and staying with me whether I'd wanted him to or not. But this wasn't his bed.

Riley ignored me as he touched the splintered wood of the closet door. "And my closet?"

"I shot up my bed and my closet," I insisted. Seriously, my Girl Scouts weren't this obtuse. "Wait, you've been here for a couple of hours already. How did you miss this?"

He shrugged. "I stayed in the living room and watched you."

"Gee, that's not at all creepy." I rolled my eyes.

So I walked through the room, explaining everything to Riley—especially the part that I didn't understand about how the killer had gotten out. He wandered around, touching everything as he listened.

"And you thought I'd killed him?" he asked.

I nodded. "I'd seen you around and knew you were in town." Okay, so that's a lie. I suspected he was here, but I'd also suspected I was hallucinating. No point in telling him that though.

Riley stuck his finger in one of the bullet holes on the bed. "You really thought I was under this bed and then fired?"

"Why are you here, Riley?" I asked again.

"You could've killed me!"

"But I didn't. Quit stalling, and tell me why you thought showing up here would help you find who took your damn book!"

Riley turned his gorgeous blue eyes on me, and his charm level shot up to fifty. But it wasn't going to work this time.

"Alright." He held up his hands. "I thought maybe you'd taken it."

"You thought what?"

"I thought you'd taken the book. That somehow you'd found out that I'd written it and had decided to steal it."

I closed my eyes and shook my head. "If I'd known you'd written a book about my exploits, I wouldn't steal it first. I'd kick your ass first. And then I'd destroy it, and then I'd kick your ass again. How could you possibly think I'd sold it to whoever?"

He shook his head. "I didn't know what to think. I was starting to panic. You just seemed like the most logical first step."

"I didn't know anything about it! How could I know you'd do something like that?"

"I'm sure I told you that I'd always wanted to write a book," he said casually.

My jaw dropped. "I didn't know anything about that! You never told me that. And even if you had, I'd never guess that you'd betray the Agency this way. Or me!"

"I didn't betray you!" He got to his feet so that he could look me in the eye.

"It never occurred to you that you'd get into trouble with this book?"

Who was this guy? It was like I was seeing a whole new side of my former partner. He'd never told me he'd wanted to be a novelist. I'd have remembered that. And writing down classified information to publish just seemed like a rookie mistake. Not something Riley would do.

But I was tired of arguing with him. The sooner we figured this out the sooner he'd go home and I could get ready for the mud run.

"Uh-oh."

"What is it?" Riley asked.

"I have a Scout meeting in five minutes!"

He frowned. "This is a weird time to have a meeting."

I agreed. "We've got a mud run coming up the day after tomorrow, and we have a strategy session planned for tonight."

I raced to the back door, followed by Riley. I ignored him as I came around to the front of the house and started heading up the street toward the school. How had I forgotten this? It was very important to the girls.

"Mrs. Wrath!" The girls cheered as I came into the classroom where we held our meetings. We didn't usually have meetings in the evenings, but this was the night that the local Boy Scouts met here, so we had piggybacked onto that.

"Mr. Riley!" they shouted.

Kelly came forward to hug him. She'd change her tune when I told her what he'd done. Or maybe she wouldn't. She adored Riley. She probably thought Riley had done all the work in babysitting Finn earlier.

"What's going on, ladies?" Riley turned his full charm on the girls. I had to admit—he was pretty good with them. He seemed more relaxed. He'd come a long way since the first time he'd met the girls—although part of that was my fault for planting candy in his jacket pockets.

"We're gonna win the mud run!" Ava announced.

"We murdered the Boy Scouts." Inez grinned.

"Boy Scouts?" Riley asked.

"I'll explain later. Okay, girls! Let's sit in a circle. We've got a lot to do and only one hour to do it."

"Am I late?" Soo Jin Body stuck her perfect and flawless head through the door.

I glared at Kelly, who shrugged. Great.

I couldn't help but notice Riley's face light up as he saw her. I watched as the two greeted each other. I felt a little twang of...what was that...rage? Jealousy? That was ridiculous. Riley wasn't mine. In fact if he dated her, she'd be less interested in Rex. So why was I upset?

Once everyone was seated, Kelly went over the rules for the race.

"You have to be good sports," she said. "We can't let competition get the best of us."

The girls nodded solemnly as if they were taking an oath to defend America. Maybe in their little brains they were.

"I know I won't be there, but I expect a clean race and no cheating."

Riley raised his hand, which I had to admit was kind of adorable. "What's a mud run?"

The four Kaitlyns started talking at once. No, that's not right. They were making sense, but they were filling in each other's sentences like a freaky, four-headed Girl Scout.

Soo Jin stood up and unrolled a large map that she clipped to the blackboard. She waited patiently for the girls to finish then stepped up.

"I did a little surveillance yesterday." She turned to the map. "Here's the layout of the course."

It was our local camp. The girls and I knew it well. She pointed at the entrance and moved her finger up the drive to the first lodge.

"It starts here. They have a huge muddy field that we have to cross. It looks like the mud is at least a couple of inches deep. There's about fifty yards of the stuff before the first element."

I stared in amazement. It never would've occurred to me that Dr. Body would sneak into camp and scope out the course. I couldn't help but admire her gumption.

Kelly fidgeted uneasily. "Isn't this cheating?"

Twelve little heads turned to glare at my co-leader, but Soo Jin smiled.

"They had a huge campout this weekend. Two teenagers got hurt. The on-call doctor at the hospital came down with pneumonia, so I volunteered to go." She smiled. "And the course parallels the drive throughout camp, so I couldn't help but see the course."

"Are the kids okay?" Kelly asked in her nurse voice.

The coroner nodded. "They fell out of a tree. Only one broken arm. They're fine."

"Go on!" Betty shouted.

Our perpetually impatient kid, Betty was also our go-to for dirty work. She'd make a great spy someday. If they took junior agents at the CIA, I'd have recommended her already.

Soo Jin made sure Kelly was satisfied before continuing. "The first obstacle is a set of ropes hanging from a wooden frame. You have to swing across—over more mud—to get to the other side. Then you run for about one hundred yards and hit the archery course."

Ugh. Archery. The last thing I wanted was my girls near any sort of pointy missile.

Kelly frowned. "The girls aren't old enough to do archery. They have to be in fourth grade for that."

Dr. Body grinned. "They aren't doing archery there. They're putting on snowshoes."

Snowshoes? Unless I'm wrong, snowshoes work best in snow. It was September—still warm, sunny days with no hope for snow anytime soon.

"Once you have the snowshoes on, you have to walk across a balance beam—over more mud."

I had to admit, I liked where this was going. And we had an advantage because we'd done a weekend at camp last winter, and the girls had done a little snowshoeing of their own. We knew how to put the shoes on. I was willing to bet that this was an advantage we would have over the other teams.

"After the balance beam," Soo Jin continued, "we take off the snowshoes and run straight up the berm at the archery area and down the other side."

Kelly interrupted. "You seem to have more information than someone who just drove through camp."

That's my best friend—always worried we'll get busted for cheating. Once, in high school, we had "accidentally" found a copy of an algebra midterm. Turned out later that it wasn't much of an advantage—Mr. Beenk had been using the same test every year for twenty years. Parents had handed the test down to their kids for two decades. (He wasn't a very popular teacher). It still bothered Kelly though. She was going to turn herself in, but I'd stopped her by telling her that she'd be screwing over generations to come if she did that, and Mr. B would probably be angry because he'd be forced to rewrite the test. Seeing how the man was sixty-five, she decided not to say anything.

"Oh," Soo Jin said, "well, once I got home, I found one of the brochures for the contestants in my purse. Accidentally."

I was impressed. And now I was glad the medical examiner was on our team.

"Then we run another fifty yards to another mud pit with beams crisscrossed over it. We have to crawl beneath the beams, through the mud, to get to the other side."

The camp was definitely going all out on this mud thing. Throw in some leeches and a few caimans, and I'd feel like that time I was in Nicaragua.

"Next we run to the canoes, where three people get into each canoe and two people push and pull it over the grass."

"That's not going to be easy," I muttered. "These girls can't pull a canoe filled with people."

Soo Jin nodded. "This is one area where we're really going to need a strategy. The way I see it, there are ten girls and two adults." She pointed at me and herself. "With five people to a canoe, we're going to need everyone."

"Could we disguise a pony as a girl? A pony could pull the canoe," Caterina suggested

"What if we motorized them somehow?" Hannah Number One asked.

"I think we should be taking steroids to pump up," Emily said softly.

"Or," I interjected before they started plotting murder to tip the balance, "we could just make sure one adult is on each canoe. Then both canoes could have one adult pushing or pulling."

"That's a great idea!" Lauren shouted. "Mr. Riley can come too!"

The girls started shrieking, and if I didn't know any better, I'd say Riley looked touched to be included.

"Mr. Riley," I said as I held my hand up in the quiet sign, "probably won't be there."

"I'll be there," he said simply.

The girls squealed, and it took a few minutes to quiet them down.

"Well, we can talk about that later," I said quickly. The last thing I needed was Riley there when he was supposed to be solving our problem. "Please continue, Dr. Body."

"After we've dragged the canoes, we'll come to a huge wall. The goal is to get everyone up and over the wall."

"That's easy!" one of the Kaitlyns said. "We've done that a million times at camp."

Okay, it was more like we had done it once, but I admired her enthusiasm.

"It's another area we need to strategize over," Kelly said.

"After that," Soo Jin added, "we just run all the way down to the lake for the paddleboard race. Then we're done!"

She looked like she'd just explained how to play Candy Land.

"The girls are too young for paddleboards." Kelly made another lame attempt to be a responsible adult.

"They've waived that requirement, and they'll have lifeguards on the water," Soo Jin responded.

"At least if we fall into the lake," I added, "that'll clean the mud off."

"I like it!" Riley clapped his hands together. "How do we get ready for this?"

I gave him a you-aren't-going glare, but he avoided my eyes.

"I still think that knowing this all in advance is a little unfair…" Kelly made her last pitch, but we all ignored her.

"And," the doctor continued, "I know who the other teams are."

"Aren't they other Girl Scout troops?" Hannah Number Two asked. Which was good, because I was wondering if she'd fallen asleep.

"Are they otters?" Lauren asked.

No one commented because it seemed like a reasonable question.

"It's mostly girls. But—" Soo Jin held up one finger. "There's one team that will be out for our blood."

"Why?" I asked. "We don't know any other troops. Who'd want to get us?"

The lovely doctor's eyes settled on one of the Kaitlyns.

"You don't mean…" the girl said and gasped.

"Yup. Brian Miller's troop is competing. Your brother."

Great. They really would be out for our blood. And I was pretty sure Brian would cheat and find ways to injure the girls. He couldn't lose twice to a bunch of little kids. And then I'd have to kill him and dispose of the body. Brian Miller was a pain in the butt.

"Who's Brian Miller?" Riley asked.

CHAPTER ELEVEN

The girls all started speaking at once until Kelly raised her hand in the quiet sign. She got to her feet and walked over to a TV with a DVD player on a cart. After plugging everything in, she turned it on.

You know, I should've been embarrassed to be so gleeful about watching us beat that troop. Soo Jin and I were adults. I guess we should've tried to stop laughing. But Brian and his band of teenage boys had got what they deserved.

During the laser tag game, I could hardly see in the darkness, but the camera had some sort of night vision capability, and I saw everything in bright green. Just as I'd suspected, the boys were completely oblivious. They played a tactical game. They played the way it should be played. Hell, they made the Navy SEALs look like, well, Boy Scouts.

But they'd underestimated us. And that had led to their downfall.

Riley was hypnotized by the whole thing. He laughed throughout but didn't take his eyes off the television once. He watched us crush those older boys, and I think he looked a bit proud of it.

"That's amazing!" He smiled when it was over. "You guys did great! You'd all make excellent Special Forces soldiers!"

The girls weren't easily dazzled by charm, but this time Riley had them enthralled. I remembered how the girls had dressed up for the guy who ran the game. Now I knew these children were entering their boy-crazy years. At least they didn't want to impress Brian Miller.

"Those guys aren't going to let you win," Riley said as his enthusiasm started to subside. "You'll have to fight for every inch on that course."

The Scouts nodded solemnly. They knew what was up. We had to win. Not just for the prize but to keep our status as champions.

"So," Kelly said as she rejoined the circle, "we have a few things to figure out. But I don't want you to break the rules. I want you to win fair and square."

Emily, who was sitting next to my co-leader, patted her on the shoulder. "It's alright, Mrs. Albers. We won't break the rules…"

But we might have to bend them. Just a little…

We decided to get together the next day, to give us all a little time to think about the course. And also because I still had the CIA breathing down my back, two murders to solve, and an evil screenwriter to take out.

"Kelly's right," Riley said as we walked back to Rex's house. I was taking him down the back alley so that we wouldn't be seen.

"About the cheating?" I asked as my eyes scanned in all directions.

"That doesn't mean we can't use certain measures to help us."

"There is no 'us.' You aren't going."

That's when I noticed that he had the brochure Soo Jin had "accidentally" found in her purse.

"Did you steal that from the good doctor?"

He smiled. "She gave it to me because I asked for it."

I let it go. There was too much going on to worry about this silly mud run. Maybe it was a good idea to have Riley help the team. Another brain trained by espionage couldn't hurt any.

We let ourselves in through Rex's back door. It was getting late, and my boyfriend would be back soon. And that was when I realized that I had no idea where Riley had been living all this time.

"Where are you staying? At the Radisson?"

He shook his head. "I've been living in the SUV and taking showers at the Y."

"You what?" Riley didn't live in cars. Even in the field he'd had the best hotel rooms. Now he was slumming it like a homeless guy?

"You heard me."

He looked at me expectantly, and I knew what he wanted. He wanted an invitation to stay here. But this wasn't my house. And I had the only guest room. Rex wasn't very happy with me right now, so I was pretty sure that I wouldn't be bunking with him in his room. And Riley wasn't sharing the guest bed with me.

I tossed him the keys to my house. "You can have the guest room at my place since you're so keen to call it your bed anyway."

From the look on his face, I couldn't tell if he was going to argue with me or kiss me. I shuddered a little inside. But after a moment he stuffed the keys into his back pocket.

"I'll need a lift to my car," he said as he headed toward the kitchen.

I didn't follow him into the kitchen. Instead, I pulled out my cell to see if Zeke had called back. He had. The voice mail said to call him in two hours. That was enough time to take Riley to what I assumed would be the black SUV he always rented.

Men's voices came from the kitchen, and I walked in to see Rex and Riley speaking. I kissed my boyfriend, and it made me feel better. Something about the detective still made me a little weak in the knees. When this was all over, I'd have to give in a little on our commitment issues. On *my* commitment issues.

"Any news?"

Rex looked frustrated. Tired. "The feds are clamping down on the investigation. I can't make a move without consulting with them."

"Have they told you anything about Pinter?" Seemed like they should trade intel, but I was pretty sure they wouldn't. The FBI and CIA didn't share their toys or play nice with regular police.

"Nothing. They keep telling me it's classified while at the same time expecting me to solve the case without any information on who I'm investigating."

"The Agency won't give you one inch," Riley said.

"They don't know that you're here." Rex gave him a look I couldn't decipher. "I'm not going to tell them, but maybe you should. You could get info that I can't."

Riley shook his head. "Bad idea. They don't like it when their agents go rogue."

"Zeke called." I just remembered. "I'll take Riley to pick up his car, and then we can call him back."

Rex's eyes narrowed. "Where are you staying?"

Riley very casually threw his thumb over his shoulder in the direction of my house. "Wrath's guest room."

While I was glad he finally acknowledged that it was mine, I was more relieved to see Rex relax over this information.

"Anything new on Dewey?" I asked.

Rex sighed. "No. And I can't understand it. That guy had no business being involved in this."

"Maybe someone just gave him a few hundred bucks to watch me?"

"That's a possibility," Rex agreed. "But why would he have the poster for *Spy Diary*? You aren't on it. There's nothing to tie you to it. It doesn't make any sense."

"Maybe it just doesn't make sense," I said. "Maybe Dewey's stoner brain couldn't do much more than make change for pizza."

"That's true. Your idea could have merit. Could be Pinter paid Dewey to keep an eye on things until he got here. He probably knew your habit of ordering pizza."

I nodded. "I do love pizza."

"Love it?" Riley laughed. "With you it's a food group."

I rolled my eyes. "So here's all we know. Dewey is shot in your driveway. He has the movie poster. He's just a slacker pizza guy with no history of doing…well…anything ever. And then Pinter shows up, breaks into my house, and is killed in my guest room. He has the screenplay. He knows where I live, and he's ex-CIA, so he somehow managed to track the movie to me."

Rex dropped the screenplay on the table next to Riley, along with some rubber gloves. The whole thing was in a leather binder with *Spy Diary* embossed in gold on the cover.

"They don't know I have this."

My eyes lit up when I saw the mysterious script. I'd really have to make it up to Rex for "borrowing" it. When this was all over, I'd think of some way to thank him for taking such a huge risk.

I continued, "We know someone allegedly took Riley's manuscript and turned it into a screenplay that was produced by Flying Bicycle Productions. So we have two murders and a movie. The murders are only connected to me by the movie. Which leads back to you…" I glared at Riley.

He was engrossed in the script. "Hey! Look at this! They used my book almost word for word!"

The man grinned like he'd won the lottery. The minute he saw that I was less than amused, he cleared his throat and set the script on the table.

"I guess I can look at this later."

"Come on. I'll take you to your car."

This whole thing was a mixed-up mess. And Riley started it by writing a book. Who knew that he'd written it? He wasn't stupid enough to mention this at work. At least I didn't think he was. But then, I didn't think he'd be stupid enough to write it in the first place, so what did I know?

I should call Maria. This whole thing left a bad taste in my mouth, but I needed to know more. Rex's hands were tied. Riley had lied to me about this book and hidden from me in my own town. I wasn't sure I trusted him enough to include him. On the other hand, I didn't want to get Maria in trouble. I really didn't want that.

Later tonight I'd call her. When I was sure she'd be home. By not calling her at work, the chance that I'd get her in trouble was reduced. Then I remembered that she'd said she'd call before any agents got here. But she hadn't. Rex said the feds were at the station. Why hadn't she let me know?

Now I was starting to worry. Had Maria been busted? The Agency wouldn't take too kindly to her slipping me intel. Dammit! This was all Riley's fault. If he hadn't written that book in the first place…

And what was wrong with him? None of his recent actions were like him. The Riley I'd known wouldn't have compromised us with a book. Hell, I didn't even know he could write! I had to check out the screenplay before Rex took it back the next day.

My former handler and boyfriend (we'd dated for like a minute a long time ago) was acting bizarrely. The suave, confident, get-out-of-any-situation-with-a-smile Riley had vanished. Granted, he'd been through a lot in the last year—mostly due to me—but this man was a professional spy. He had never done anything that wasn't by the book. So why write a book now?

That was disturbing. Maria might be getting fired as we speak, and Riley was AWOL from the Agency.

"You ready?" Riley dragged me out of my thoughts.

"Let's go," I answered. In minutes we were in the car, headed to Marlowe's Grocery Store.

"I parked around back," Riley said as we pulled up.

Of course he had. No one parked there but maybe a few employees.

And he could walk. I stayed in front of the store.

"I want to read the script," I said as he unbuckled his seat belt.

To my surprise, Riley flushed a deep red. I'd never known him to blush before.

"Well," he said very slowly as he measured his words, "I think I should go through it first. Just to see how closely it follows the book."

"Seriously? I saw the movie. It certainly followed my life. Which means it followed your book."

"Not everything was in the movie."

"Well—!" I exclaimed as I threw my hands up in the air. "They only have ninety minutes. They'd have to cut some things out."

Riley opened the door and stepped out. He shut the door quickly and started walking away.

"Hey! What's been taken out?" I shouted through my window.

He either didn't hear me or ignored me. My guess was the latter. I followed him back to Rex's, the question still on my tongue. What was removed? What was he hiding? Maybe he made me a villain? Or maybe he just doesn't want me to see what he wrote. That thought set off alarm bells in my head.

Riley and I both parked in the alley behind Rex's house. That would have to change. I had a little hidden alley behind my house where he'd have to put his car. Mine was the only house on the street that had access, and it was hidden behind some very large bushes.

"What do you think they took out?" I held the house key out of his reach.

"Nothing. It's nothing." He grabbed for them, but I pulled back.

"You have one hour to read it. Then I'm coming to get it. This is not negotiable." I removed the house key and handed it to him.

"Are you going to change the bullet-riddled sheets?"

I turned toward Rex's back door and called out over my shoulder, "Clean sheets are in the linen closet. Change them yourself. One hour, Riley. You have one hour. And if you're not there, I'm calling the CIA to tell them everything."

I didn't wait to hear his response. He knew I had him. If he skipped out with the script, he'd become the investigation. I didn't really want to do that because if he didn't replace the manuscript in the morning, Rex would be in some serious trouble.

"You're back." Rex met me in the kitchen and handed me a glass of wine.

"Thanks." I swallowed it in one gulp. "I needed that. I'm heading over to my house in an hour. Something tells me I need to read that script. And I want to make sure you get it back."

Rex agreed. "Good idea."

He pulled me into his arms and gave me a long, satisfying kiss. Could it be that he wasn't mad at me anymore? That would be nice. Maybe we could go upstairs and...

Oh wait.

"I have to call Zeke." I pulled away. "Hold that thought, okay?"

Rex kissed my forehead. "I'll be upstairs. But don't wait too long. I'm beat."

I watched him and his perfect butt as he walked up the stairs. I was pretty sure I could take care of this and sneak in a little make-out session before heading over to my house.

Zeke answered on the first ring.

"Finn." He sounded odd. "No time for pleasantries."

"What did you find out?"

"I met the agents at Spago. It was pretty funny seeing all fourteen guys standing there, embarrassed to see each other."

"Send me the video," I said and laughed.

"Anyway, after insisting these guys tell me what's going on or I'd send some compromising videos I had to Langley, they wouldn't shut up."

"That's good."

"It seems that the CIA is convinced you're behind this. They're building a case to have you arrested for leaking classified info. The problem is that they can't tie you to the movie. They've got nothing. But they're looking, believe me."

"Fantastic." I sighed. If the Agency wanted to put me away, they weren't above creating the things they needed to do that. They could fabricate proof if they couldn't find it.

"Any chance you could slip away to the Caymans?" It didn't sound like Zeke was joking.

I could do that. I had enough money to drop everything and run away. And a year ago I might have done just that. But things had changed now. I had Rex. I had my troop. And I was the godmother of Kelly's baby. Leaving all of that wasn't an option I was willing to consider.

"Can't," I said dejectedly.

"I'll see what I can do," Zeke said. "I know you didn't do this."

"You do?" Well, that was good.

"You're not that stupid."

Good thing he couldn't see me wince. Zeke didn't know Riley was responsible. It would be so easy to say that and let him tell the others. I pictured Riley in my house, reading. We had a history together, professional and romantic. I couldn't throw him to the wolves just yet.

Oh yes, I was considering it. I know that sounded mean, but this was his fault. His mistake. And he was making me look bad by being out here.

"Anything on Flying Bicycle Productions or Black Ops Productions?" I asked.

"I found an address for both and stopped by. It's an empty office in a strip mall. The place was so clean that I wonder if they aren't spies themselves."

Well, that was just great.

"Okay. Thanks, Zeke. I really appreciate it."

"Not a problem." He hung up before I could respond.

I called Maria. It was late here in Iowa and even later on the East Coast.

A robotic female voice answered. "This line has been disconnected."

Disconnected? This was Maria's personal cell number. That was really bad. What happened to her to make her do that? Was she persona non grata at the CIA? Why get rid of her personal number? It didn't make any sense.

This was a dilemma. After hesitating a few moments, I called her office number.

It rang. And rang. And rang. The call didn't go to voice mail. There was no automated answering machine giving options. It just rang.

This was bad. Very, very bad. Something had happened to Maria. And I was in no position to help her.

CHAPTER TWELVE

"Riley!" I slammed the kitchen door to the garage behind me. "Riley!"

He appeared in the hallway, wearing pajama pants and nothing else. A light, golden fuzz rippled across his tan and muscular chest. I tried to swallow but couldn't. Riley was beyond handsome. No matter how you felt about him, when you saw him undressed, he took your breath away.

"Maria's missing," I finally said and explained what happened.

He frowned. "That's not good. What did Zeke say?"

"Riley, Maria is missing. I have no way to contact her. That's freaking me out right now."

"Maria is an exceptional agent, Merry." He moved closer to me. He smelled like soap. I loved the smell of soap.

"Don't worry about her. What did Zeke say?"

"That the CIA is convinced I did this." I filled him in on Zeke's investigation into the production company.

But all I could think about was Maria. My imagination was going crazy as I pictured her in a cinder-block cell, a bare lightbulb overhead. Yes, I know that's a cinematic cliché, but it just happens to be real.

"That's good," Riley said. "They don't know about me."

"That's good?" My blood pressure spiked. "It's good that I'm getting blamed for something you did? You selfish bastard!"

"Whoa." Riley held his hands up. "That's not what I meant. I meant they aren't any closer to the truth. That means they aren't ready to act. That means we have time to deal with this."

I shook my head. "You deal with this. My life is messed up right now because of you. I'd like things to go back to normal. Maybe I should just call Langley and let them know what really happened."

He rolled his eyes. He actually rolled his eyes. "I think you're overreacting."

"Oh yeah? Well, Maria has vanished, this town is overflowing with men in black suits, and I am probably going to prison for something I didn't do. Two men are dead over this. You still think I'm overreacting?"

I was shouting, so yeah, I was probably overreacting.

"It's going to be alright." Riley took a step closer and pulled me into his arms.

I pushed away. "Don't try to use your charms on me! I know you too well!"

"I was just trying to…"

I barely heard him because I was halfway down the hall. Once I hit the guest room, I scooped up the script.

"This—" I said as I held up the thick clump of papers, "is about my career. I'm taking it. You'd better start making some phone calls or something. I want you to have this solved tomorrow."

Pushing past him, I stormed out of my house and back to Rex's. After letting myself in, I slumped against the door. Why was I shaking? Was this outrage? Fear? Confusion? Riley was really doing a number on me.

Locking up, I moved through the house, closing curtains. Upstairs Rex was sound asleep. Philby and Martini gave me accusatory glares, as I looked through the door, before snuggling back against him. Gingerly, I closed his door and went into the guest room where I got ready for bed.

As I leaned back against my pillow, I started to read. The script was pretty much like what I'd seen on the screen. My guts twisted as I read about my own missions. It was hard to see myself laid out in black and white. And they had me making stupid decisions and screwing up. Was that from the screenwriter or had Riley done that too? I read quickly until I got halfway through the script.

A page was marked up with a red pen. It looked like they'd taken something out after all. Another character. Rigby.

My eyes narrowed. Riley had written himself into the story. Rigby was the main character's handler. She was blonde and hot, and the guy spy was completely in her thrall. That's when I realized I'd never noticed the spy's name. Throughout the script, he was just listed as *Spy*. That was weird. He should've had a name, right?

Oh well, what did it matter? It looked like they'd cut the whole story line about Rigby. At least they hadn't crossed it out.

Rigby is confident and smart. Spy understands he's being seduced but can't help falling in love with his handler.

What?

Then I read the most explicit love scene I'd ever read in a book or anything. Yes, I read, but not stuff like this. I could feel the heat rising from my toes to my face. It was far too personal. Too scorching hot. Too familiar...

I set the script down and stared into space for a bit. Then I re-read it.

That's why Riley didn't want me to see it. In his book and in this script, even though it was edited out, Riley had the characters engaged in a love affair that was exactly like the one he and I had had back in Japan. He hadn't just written about my career—he'd included my love life.

It almost hurt to continue reading. I bounced it off the wall. A few times.

In Riley's story he and I were madly, passionately in love. And we had a ridiculous amount of sex. That was all fiction. But we also didn't break up—like we actually had just a few weeks into our romance. In fact Rigby and Spy were planning to spend the rest of their lives together.

Why would he write that? Was that what he wanted? Was he still carrying a torch for me? And what was I going to do about that?

Nothing, that's what. This was just Riley's little fantasy. There was no basis in fact. And it certainly wasn't important. It wasn't what was in the script—it was that it existed at all. Besides, the Agency wouldn't give a damn about any romance.

They were worried that the sensitive information regarding my past cases was out for all the world to see.

Oh no. Rex! Had he read it? If he had, why didn't he tell me?

A chill ran up my spine. Over the past two years Riley had inserted himself between Rex and me a few times. And while I was pretty sure things were over between us, I still had a little spark flickering in my stomach.

This wasn't getting me anywhere closer to the truth. It was just one more distraction. I still had no idea who had stolen Riley's book and made it into a movie. I still didn't know why I was being watched by a stoner pizza delivery dude, and I hadn't discovered why Tim Pinter had been in my house, or who had killed him or Dewey.

Argh!

And now I had to worry that Rex had read this and realized how Riley obviously felt about me. Wait. Did Riley still feel that way?

I shook my head to clear it. I had to stay focused. None of that mattered. I had more important things to worry about. Maria for one. The mud run for another. Why did solving this matter to me? Oh right. Because the CIA thought I was behind this.

Time to call it a night. I could worry about everything else in the morning.

CHAPTER THIRTEEN

"Hey you!" Rex kissed me as he came into the kitchen, being far more chipper than the situation warranted.

I'd been sitting at the kitchen table for an hour, staring into space. And I still wasn't any closer to knowing what was going on.

"Any big plans for the day?" Rex asked.

For a second his eyes darted toward the living room, which I took to mean my house and its obnoxious guest. Oh, he'd read it alright.

"I'm going to go for a jog." I stretched my arms up over my head and immediately regretted it because it hurt. Two years out of the field and I was seriously out of shape.

"You alright?" he asked when I winced.

"Oh yeah. Just a little leg cramp."

"Leg cramp when you're stretching your arms?"

"Sure. What else?" Covered that like a boss!

"Okay." He saw that I'd made him coffee and took the cup from the machine. "Just be careful."

I promised as he left. The second the door was closed, I took three ibuprofen. Too bad the stuff didn't work instantly.

It was a fantastic day with an early autumn warmth that made me feel a little better. Okay, now I was outside. Where would I go? The mud run was only one day away, and as I started running, I instantly regretted signing up for it. I can run short distances, and I'm a track star when I'm being chased by anyone with a chain saw. But jogging didn't appear to come naturally to me.

Two blocks away, I was bent over and panting. Why didn't I start getting into shape when we first knew about this?

Well, nothing for it now. The girls were counting on me. I stood up and decided to power walk instead.

Now this was more like it. I could do this for at least four blocks. As I moved, my muscles started to loosen up. Could I power walk the course? From what Soo Jin said, there was going to be one long run down to the lake.

The terrain in camp would be in my favor because, as I remembered it, that route was all downhill. Surely I could run downhill easily enough. That was just gravity. It'd be more like falling down a hill while upright.

I stopped again. This time I panted a little less, and I took that as a small victory. I was at least six or seven blocks from Rex's house. Someone else was out running. In the distance I saw a man running toward me. No way could I let someone see me like this, so I propped my leg up on a little rock wall and pretended to stretch.

The man was getting closer, although still a couple of blocks away. He appeared to be smiling. Great. It was Riley. That was all I needed. I finally got a little alone time, and he came along.

With the sigh of a thousand martyrs, I straightened up and pasted a smile on my face. Not sure if it was even remotely sincere, but that was how I was feeling. Riley slowed down to a walk, not even out of breath, dammit.

I waved, indicating it was okay for him to join me. This whole jogging disaster had lasted only a few minutes. Riley's expression began to change. He was frowning—and he didn't like doing that because it encouraged wrinkles. He suddenly started speeding up and running toward me.

Rough arms grabbed me from behind, and I smashed the back of my head into the front of the head of whoever had grabbed me. I heard groaning, and another guy stepped in front of me. I was just about to knock him senseless when the whole world went black.

* * *

"Wake up, princess," a deep voice growled.

"It's a little tough to do when tied to a chair and blindfolded," I responded.

Seriously—tied to a chair? Is that the best these guys could do?

"I think we'll keep the blindfold on a little longer," the voice said. "And the ropes too. You broke my nose, you know."

The throbbing in the back of my head was worth it.

"Who are you, and what do you want?" It was really a long shot to ask that. Any smart bad guy wouldn't tell you anything. That was just in the movies.

"The script," the same man answered.

"The script? I'm not sure what you're talking about."

"The one your boyfriend brought home from work."

Oh. That script. As far as I knew, it was still there. Unless Rex had it hidden on his person when he had left this morning, and judging from the fact that he was wearing khaki slacks and a fitted shirt, I was pretty sure it was still there.

"Why do you want it?"

Why didn't they just break in and get it after I'd left? It's not like I'd taken it jogging with me. And what did they want it for?

"Is it back at the house?" the voice asked.

I shook my head. "Rex took it back to the station with him this morning. The feds didn't want it out of their sight."

There was a fair amount of swearing, but I heard two distinct voices.

"Did you steal Riley's book?" I asked. "And then you wrote the script? It was all onscreen, so why do you need it?"

One of my captors cleared his throat. "We just do."

His voice was high and squeaky. It took all I had in me not to laugh.

"You'll have to go to the police and plead your case, then, because that's where it is."

Why did I lie? Because I hadn't finished reading it yet and didn't want them to go to Rex's house. A chill ran through me. What if they did anyway? Would they hurt my cats? Because I'd have to take a finger for every hair they harmed on Philby and Martini.

"Did you read it?" The guy sounded like he'd inhaled helium.

I shook my head. "I was going to. But Rex said he had to get it back. The CIA wants to take possession."

There was the scrape of a chair on concrete, and I thought I detected a slight echo. We were in some warehouse or barn or something. There were a lot of those around, with this being a farming community and all.

"So good luck with that," I added.

An argument broke out between the two men, and I tried to wriggle my wrists. Not zip ties. These guys used actual scratchy rope. I heard snippets of "you idiot!" and "everything screwed up!" And I thought I heard something about llama milk, but that might have been wrong.

The ropes were too coarse and tight. These guys knew what they were doing. My ankles were a little more loosely tied to each of the front legs of the chair. I strained to touch the chair to figure out if it was wood or metal. Metal. Damn. And me without my portable blowtorch.

The air changed around me as someone moved in close and slapped me hard against the face. I didn't cry out, just straightened my head.

"You moron! Don't hit her in the face!" Squeaky said.

There was a brief pause before I heard the other guy ask why not.

"Because she's our only way into the station. And she's going to steal it for us. And if her face is all bruised up, the cops will know something's up before she even says anything."

"You want me to go into the police station and swipe the script? Is that right?" I asked.

This would be my method of escape. These guys were rubes.

"Sure. I can do that," I lied. "I even know where Rex is keeping it. I can have it in your hands in five minutes."

Yeesh. Bad guys sure weren't what they used to be. The second I was in there, I'd be better protected than Fort Knox.

Laughter broke out. Sinister laughter. Like the laughter in a James Bond movie.

"I'm thinking you are thinking that this is your ticket out of here," Gruff said.

He was close. I could smell sweat and bad breath. As much as I wanted to smash my forehead into his nose, I wouldn't do it. There was no point in doing anything that might change the plan.

"You think we're stupid?" Squeaky asked. "We've been watching you and your house."

Yes, I did.

"No."

And that's when I heard it. A low meow. It sounded familiar, but how could I be sure?

"Bobb!" I shouted, repeating the name of a man who a while ago had tried to kill her.

The hiss practically shook the building. Damn it. They had Philby. I guess they weren't so stupid after all.

CHAPTER FOURTEEN

"You hurt my cat," I snarled, "and you'll regret it. I'll hunt you down and destroy you."

"We won't hurt your cat, if you bring us the script," Squeaky said.

This was a no-brainer. As far as I'd seen, there wasn't anything in the script. Besides, I didn't care if these guys had it. Sure, I wanted to know why they needed it but not bad enough to jeopardize Philby.

"So let's do this," I said evenly.

A familiar object jabbed me in the shoulder. These guys had a gun. Of course they did.

"Don't try anything stupid," Gruff said as someone untied my ankles.

"Don't worry, I won't. Take off the blindfold, will you? I won't be able to walk."

"No, sweetheart," Squeaky said. "We're keeping the blindfold on. At least till we get to the station."

Fine. Whatever. Now I had a different problem. In order to save my cat, I had to give them the script. Right now these guys thought it was at the police station—because that was what I'd told them.

Except it wasn't at the police station. It was at Rex's house. And that was where Martini was. These guys were either lying about having the cat, or they searched the house and were too stupid to find the script.

Regardless, if I told them the truth, I ran the risk of something happening to Martini, or I'd get roughed up because 1) I'd lied and 2) they didn't need my pretty face anymore.

However, sticking with the lie meant I'd have to figure something out once I got into the station. Was it possible that they'd made a copy of the script? I wasn't sure I should pin my hopes on that.

And where the hell was Riley? He'd witnessed my kidnapping. He knew what they looked like and had probably chased their car a ways. Why isn't he breaking down the damn door with an Uzi?

I was on my own. I could stall and wait for the aforementioned rescue, but it might not come for a while. Besides, I wanted to give those jerks what they wanted so that I could take my cat and go home.

"Now that I think about it," I said slowly, licking my dry lips. "I didn't see Rex take the script this morning. It's probably back at his house."

I didn't flinch in anticipation of a punch in the face. But I didn't care. It was more important to me to get Philby back by giving them exactly what they wanted than to keep my pretty face intact.

Silence. I figured it would take them a moment to realize I'd lied. No matter. I'd been hit in the face before. I knew what to expect, and I didn't want these guys to think I was scared.

"Are we going or what?" I asked. "Philby needs her medicine."

Someone helped me to my feet while jamming the gun into my ribs.

"Let's go. Remember, be cool."

"No problem. Philby comes with. I give you the script, and you leave me and my cat alone."

"Fine," Squeaky said.

I was hustled to a car and shoved into the back seat.

"Let me see my cat so that I know you're going to live up to your end of the deal," I snapped.

The weight of a furry bowling ball with legs was tossed onto my lap. As usual, Philby curled up and went to sleep.

At least one of us wasn't worried.

I guesstimated the time it took to drive to the house. I figured about ten minutes. That meant we'd still been in town when they'd slapped me around. My mind worked furiously. Did

Rex keep a gun in the house? It wasn't too far-fetched. Lots of law enforcement, military, and ex-feds did.

The problem was, I'd never seen one. Now if we were going to my house, I'd be able to get to the Glock in the kitchen behind the wineglasses or the shotgun behind the couch. But we weren't going to my house. And once I delivered the script and saw that Philby was safe, I wanted to shoot them.

"Who's the guy?" Gruff asked.

"The guy?" I asked.

"Yeah, the handsome blond guy who chased us down the street. The one you were smiling at before we grabbed you."

Squeaky asked, "You thought he was handsome?"

"Yeah. Why?"

"That's just a weird thing to say about another man."

"I had to describe him in a way that she'd know who I was talking about." Gruff sounded a little defensive.

"You could've said 'blond guy.' You didn't have to say 'handsome.'"

Gruff sounded angry. "You describe him your way, and I'll describe him mine. And I chose the word *handsome*."

"Whatever," Squeaky said. "It's just bizarre, that's all."

Those two weren't going to win the Nobel Prize anytime soon.

"Would you describe me as handsome?"

Gruff grumbled, "No. You are anything but handsome. I'd say you look more like a ferret."

Ha! I was right. I'd guessed the high-pitched voice was weasel-like. Wisely, I kept this opinion to myself.

"A ferret?" Ferret-face screeched. "Well, you look like one of them gorillas!"

So Gruff was big and bulky. Good to know. It's amazing the intel you can get just by listening to someone talk. If they kept this up, I'd have their social security numbers soon.

The car came to a stop, and I wondered if we were in the driveway in front or the alley in back. Either way, hopefully Riley was watching. As long as he didn't put Philby in danger, I didn't care what he'd do to these idiots.

Someone removed my blindfold. Wow. They really did look like a gorilla and ferret. I immediately averted my eyes. Not because I was afraid. I just didn't want to give them a reason to kill Philby and me.

Gorilla got out of the car and pulled me out of the back seat while Ferret snatched up Philby, while still holding the gun on me.

We were in the alley. That made sense. It was broad daylight. They'd draw attention waving a gun around in the middle of the day.

"*Hey!*" Elmer from next door waddled out onto his deck and looked at us over the fence. "*You rotten kids! Quit screwing around out there!*"

He shook his fist, and his pants fell down. We watched as he waddled back inside, pants around his ankles. He looked like a deranged penguin.

"That guy saw us!" Ferret squealed.

Gorilla shrugged. "He was stone deaf. That's why he shouted. And he thought we were kids. So I'm guessing he can't see. Don't worry about him."

I led the way to the back door and unlocked it with the key I'd had in my pocket when I'd left this morning to jog. Who knew I'd end up kidnapped and leading a couple of goons into Rex's house not an hour later? At least, I thought it was an hour.

"Don't try anything," Ferret said, putting the gun to Philby's head.

"Hey," Gorilla said. "If you hold the gun like that and it goes off, you'll shoot yourself in the arm."

My blood pressure was spiking. They'd gone too far now.

Ferret pointed the gun at me. "You realize that your cat looks like Hitler, right?"

I didn't say anything as I led them through the living room to the stairs. As we climbed, I toyed with turning around and kicking both of them, but Ferret still had Philby. So I didn't.

"Okay," Gorilla grumbled. "So it's okay for you to compare her cat to Hitler, but I can't call a guy handsome?"

"What? The cat looks like Adolf Hitler! That's a good description. You could've said the guy looked like someone famous."

"Well, he doesn't look like anyone famous," Gorilla said. "Which is why I went with handsome."

"Yes, he does. He looks like that guy on that show I like. The one with the dolphin and the doctors."

Gorilla stopped walking. "Well, I've never seen that show, so I couldn't know what you're talking about, could I?"

Anytime now, Riley. If he was smart, he'd come up behind Ferret, disarm him, and take my cat. Then I could knock Gorilla over the railing. But there was no sign of him. With my luck, he was probably out looking for me.

We walked into the guest room, and I found the script on the floor. The cover was a little beat-up from me throwing it against the wall last night. I snatched it up and held it out. Gorilla reached for it, but I pulled it back.

"I want my cat first," I said.

I was pretty certain these guys were going to shoot me just because I was a witness. But maybe I could get Philby to hide so that they wouldn't harm her. It was one hell of a long shot.

Ferret tossed Philby on the bed, and the cat bolted out of the room. Good girl.

I tossed the script to Ferret, and in his attempt to grab it, he dropped the gun. I dove under the bed to get it as it clattered to the floor. My fingers closed on it, and I pulled it back under the bed. Unfortunately, I was under the bed.

Gorilla jumped on the bed, and I fired up through the mattress. There was an *oof* sound, and when I got to my feet, the men were gone. I ran after them, but by the time I reached the alley, the car was out of range.

I tucked the gun into my waistband and went back into the house, locking the door behind me. Sirens wailed in the distance. I wondered if Elmer had heard the gunshots and called it in or whether he did it to deal with those unruly kids. He wasn't really deaf…his wife Ethel was. I decided I'd bake some cookies and send them over.

"Police!" men shouted from the living room.

I dropped the gun into an umbrella stand Rex had by the back door and walked into the room with my hands up. Officer Kevin Dooley and Rex were standing there, guns drawn. When he saw me, Rex lowered his weapon and pulled me into his arms. Kevin, on the other hand, still kept his gun trained on me until he saw a bag of chips on the dining room table.

"You're safe. When Riley came into the station and told us what happened, I was a wreck!" Rex said as he crushed me against him.

I'm a modern woman. I can take care of myself. Still, it was nice to know that Rex was there for me. Now where was Riley?

"Put the chips down, Kevin, and head back to the station." Rex released me. "Anyone still here?"

I shook my head. "They got away."

Riley arrived as I was explaining the whole thing. I walked them through the house, step by step. We ended up in the guest room where two holes darkened the middle of the bed.

"What do you have against beds?" Riley asked.

"Where were you?" I narrowed my eyes.

He actually looked hurt, which made me feel a little bad.

"Riley went straight to the station, Merry," Rex explained. "We have full descriptions of the car and its license plates because of him. We were getting ready to mount a search when we got the call that someone had heard gunshots."

I guessed Elmer had called it in.

"They took the script. Why would they want it?" I asked.

The men looked confused. "This was about the script?" Riley asked. "I never finished reading it."

Rex shook his head. "Me neither."

"Huh. I didn't get all the way through it either," I admitted. "So there could be something interesting in there after all."

Riley gave me a strange look, but I ignored it.

"So," Riley said to Rex, "you have the details on the car. You can find these guys. Or Wrath and I will."

"Oh no." I shot back. "I'm out of this. All I want to know is if Maria is okay. Then you are going to deal with this. I have a mud run to win."

"Where's your loyalty to the Agency?" Riley asked.

"I don't have any. I haven't worked there for two years. I'm retired. I don't know how many times I have to tell you that."

Philby and Martini appeared and started rubbing against my legs.

I pointed at Riley. "You are handling this. Not me. It's your book that started all of this."

"You know they won't leave you alone. They think you are behind this," Rex said.

"No one has tried to interrogate me yet. So maybe they don't actually suspect me."

That was true. For all the talk of the CIA coming to "get" me, no one had. Instead they were crawling all over LA.

"This isn't over," Riley said grimly. "I'm going to find those bastards who kidnapped you."

"Go ahead. But you'll do it without me."

We stood there, facing off. Riley and I had worked together on some serious messes in the last two years since I was retired. But now I was drawing a line in the…I looked down at the floor…hardwood.

"Fine." Riley walked out, slamming the door.

I watched as he went over to my house and walked in. Damn. While it was great that he was going to deal with this, it wasn't great that my house was going to be his base of operations. Was I ever going to get rid of this guy?

"Are you alright?" Rex asked. That's when I realized that, except for the cats, we were totally alone.

"Yes," I lied.

"I'll take the rest of the day off," Rex said as he pulled out his cell phone.

I shook my head. "No, you should go. You have a lot to do."

"Merry." He looked deep into my eyes. "Are you serious about staying out of this?"

I shrugged. "I need to know what happened to Maria. I'll talk to Zeke again, but that's it. I promise."

He seemed to consider this. "Keep your cell close. I'm not convinced that I should go back to work."

"Go. I'm fine."

He left, and I locked the door behind him. I wandered through the house, checking all the doors and windows. Would the guys come back here? They had the script, but I'd shot one of them, so they might want revenge.

I slumped onto the couch, and the cats jumped up beside me. Was I really done with this? My life had become more complicated since I'd left the Agency. Why was that? Was I a walking threat magnet? Seriously, something was off.

Through the window I could see Riley leave the house, get into his SUV, and drive off. I figured he wasn't hiding anymore. Would I really throw him to the wolves? And by wolves, I meant the CIA? Did I have it in me to do that?

I'd known Riley a long time. We had worked together side by side for years. In some pretty dangerous situations. Something told me that this was a mistake—that I wasn't being very loyal. Kicking him to the curb wasn't something Merry of two years ago would have done—mostly because we'd had more than a working relationship. In Japan we'd been romantically involved until I caught him in a clinch with another woman.

Of course, years later I found out that I'd been wrong and that Riley was still carrying a torch for me. And from the looks of the script I'd just read, he was still thinking of me in a manner that was not cool.

Riley had proved his feelings over and over by continuing to come to my aid since I'd left the Agency. None of those situations had been his fault. But this one was.

The whole mess was exhausting. I also had Rex to deal with. Deal with? I wasn't sure that was the right choice of words. Rex and I had been romantically involved for the past year and a half, and we were happy.

Well, except for the fact that he wanted me to move in. That had knocked me for a loop. And I was totally resisting that. I pulled out my cell.

Kelly answered on the second ring. I filled her in on everything. She knew about my past, and she knew what was going on with me and these two men. Maybe she'd know exactly what I should do. That would be awesome.

"Of course Riley still has feelings for you," my best friend said. "How could you not see that?"

"I don't know. Maybe I don't want to."

"And yet you're resisting Rex in taking this relationship to the next level," she said.

You know, it really was annoying how she did that.

"What's wrong with me?"

"More than I have time for in this phone call," Kelly answered.

"What should I do?"

"What do you want to do?"

"You know, that's really annoying."

"This is your life, Merry. As your friend, you can bounce stuff off of me, but I won't make decisions for you."

"How about you sum up what you think is happening?"

There was a sigh on the other end. "Okay. Well, I think you have feelings and might in fact be in love with both men."

A little explosion went off inside my brain, and I was pretty sure smoke came out of my ears because both cats looked alarmed.

"I am not!"

"Yes, you are. And until you can decide who you want and what you want, you can't move forward," Kelly said.

"That's not exactly what I was looking for when I called you."

"I know."

"How could I possibly be in love with both men? That doesn't make any sense."

"If you really think about it, it makes perfect sense. You love Rex. That's obvious. But when you found out just a few months ago that your breakup with Riley had been based on a misunderstanding, it undermined your relationship with Rex."

"Why?"

"Because you now had to figure out how you felt about Riley. My guess is that froze you in your tracks with Rex because you want to figure that out before moving on with him."

Oh wow. She was right. Kelly nailed it. I was so busy fending Rex off that I never thought about why I was doing it. This was very unfair to me. And even more unfair to the two men in my life who, for some reason, both had names that started with *R*.

"You should've been a psychologist."

"You'd keep me so busy that I wouldn't be able to take on a second client."

"I'm not that mental."

"No, you're not. You've just been through a lot in the last few years. And now you have a decision that you're not prepared to make."

I heard her doorbell ring in the background. The voice of another woman giggled in the background. I knew that voice.

"You're hanging with Dr. Body now?" I tried not to scream it into the phone.

"I have to go," Kelly said. "Bye."

She hung up before I could protest. I had just started to like the coroner. Especially since I knew she wasn't really into Rex. But now she was hanging out with my best friend? She could have both men as long as she didn't take Kelly from me.

"I'm not smart enough to deal with all of this," I said aloud.

The cats gave me a look then looked at each other before falling asleep. At least I still had these two. I'd have four, but Riley had given my other two kittens away to Soo Jin.

Try as I might, was I ever really going to like her? This made me sad. Then my stomach rumbled.

In the kitchen I made a peanut butter sandwich. As I chewed, I turned Kelly's words over in my head. Was I in love with both Riley and Rex? I knew how I felt about Rex…but Riley? She was right—I had never really resolved my feelings for him. But was I really in love with him? And was he in love with me? From the stuff in the script, I knew lust was at least a factor. But love?

That would explain why he was always here…coming to my rescue. Ugh. I hated that thought. I didn't need rescuing. I'd rescued Riley before, but he certainly didn't need to rescue me. I thought about my suddenly boy-crazy Scouts. I wondered if they made a badge for independence and not needing a man. If not, I'd have to invent one.

As to my problem, the answer was obvious. I'd choose Rex. I'd move in with Rex. And then Riley would have closure. He could move on and seduce all of Iowa. That would be the kind thing to do.

Would I just be moving in with Rex so that I could close the chapter on Riley? That hardly seemed fair. I thought about that. If I moved in here, it would have to be real. I'd have to be sure. Did I want to give up my independence just to make things easier for Riley?

Argh! No matter what I did, I'd be second-guessing myself. These problems were real. And if I ignored them, both men would go away.

Philby gave me a look before barfing on my lap.

"Why did you do that?" I asked as I grabbed some tissues from the end table.

Philby gave the cat equivalent of a shrug and ran off, presumably to reload. She wasn't giving me a chance to feel sorry for myself.

And neither was I. I called Maria's cell.

"Wrath," my friend whispered.

"You answered! Do you know how worried I've been about you?"

"Sorry about that. They're keeping a close eye on me at work. They even follow me into the bathroom."

"Who's following you?"

"Tilda King."

That was all she needed to say. Tilda King was a certified flunky of the higher-ups. An unpleasant woman on a good day, if she was suddenly hanging around you, you could be sure the bosses were spying on you.

"That sucks."

"I'm sorry I haven't called. You probably know the Agency sent some guys."

"They haven't talked to me yet. In fact, they're mostly just hanging out at the station." I didn't see any point in being angry with her.

"Maria, have you ever heard of Tim Pinter? He showed up dead in my house. I've heard he's ex-CIA."

"No. I guess I can look him up." She didn't sound like she wanted to do that.

"Don't do it if you'll get busted," I insisted.

"It's okay. I'll figure something out. I really have to go though. I'll call soon."

I was no closer to the truth, and I'd already broken my own do-this-without-me-Riley rule. I wasn't getting out of this anytime soon. I called Zeke.

"Hey Finn," Zeke answered before I'd even heard it ring. "Flying Bicycle is a film studio. But they work for Russia."

"Propaganda films." I snapped my fingers. Any film studio in Russia was for the sake of propaganda.

"That's right. My guess is that *Spy Diary* was supposed to be a smear campaign against the Agency. You were just in the way."

"What's happened to the film?"

"It sounds like every copy in the US has been seized and destroyed."

"Well, thanks, Zeke."

"That's all I can tell you right now. Sorry."

"You've been a huge help. Thank you. I'll send a case of Girl Scout cookies your way."

"Send a variety. I love them all." Zeke hung up.

So the Russians had stolen Riley's book. They had hired staff and a cast and produced the movie. But it was shut down in the middle of its first showing, so what had they achieved?

And what about Dewey and Tim? And I still had no idea how Pinter was murdered in a locked guest room. My locked guest room. What about the idiots who'd kidnapped me? Were they Russian?

It seemed like the minute we got one solution, more questions popped up. That was really annoying. I wanted it to stop.

Unfortunately, there was only one person I could talk to about this, and he'd just driven away. Maybe I should drive away too. Minnesota would be nice and cool this time of year. Why not go all the way to Canada? Take a vacation and think this through. Or not think of anything at all. That would be better.

No, that wasn't me. I couldn't stand not knowing how this ended. Yes, I now knew who'd made the movie, but not why. Had Dewey just been hired to follow me? Had Pinter tried to set me up?

Maybe Pinter had stolen the manuscript from Riley. That would mean he had been working for the Russians. I hated that.

Double agents were the worst kind of traitors. It's all about the money with them. Politics aren't important.

Ideas swirled in my head. Could it really be that simple? The Russians make a movie based on a real spy's cases in order to…what? It was hardly enough to topple the US government. It might embarrass them, but I was too awesome for that.

Gruff and Ferret were worried about something in the script. So worried that they kidnapped Philby and me to get it back. The script was proof that someone knew about Riley.

Even the Russians weren't this simple, and their plans didn't usually go awry.

Dewey, Pinter, Gruff and Ferret. Who were they, and how were they involved?

Just then, Riley's car pulled back into my driveway. From the way he walked into the house, I guessed that he hadn't found what he was looking for. My heart fluttered a little as the door shut behind him.

No time like the present. I had to go over there and tell him what I'd found out. The problem was, I didn't want to. Now that I knew that I might still have feelings for him, he was the last person I wanted to see.

My cell buzzed. *I'll bring home dinner. We need to talk.* It was Rex.

Before I could deal with that, I'd need to face Riley. And I only had a few hours to do it.

CHAPTER FIFTEEN

I never walked across the street so slowly. He could probably see me. In which case, walking very slowly was going to look weird. It was like I was making my way to the gallows. And yet, I couldn't seem to walk any faster. On the other side of the street...on the other side of the door...was Riley. And I was supposedly in love with him.

He answered the door before I put my foot on the first step. I moved a little faster because there was no point now. I felt the irony of Riley closing the door behind me—as if he lived here and I didn't.

My heart beat a little faster. Was I imagining that? It could be that I was anxious about telling him about the Russians. On the other hand, maybe that would be enough intel for him to move on.

"Flying Bicycle Productions is..." I would've finished my sentence, but Riley's mouth was on mine, and from experience, it is harder to talk with your mouth full of...someone else's mouth.

I'd be lying if I said it didn't cause some tingling. It did. Riley's arms encircled me, and his hands ran down the length of my back. By this time, I was kissing him back. It felt good. Too good.

"I can't." I pushed away. "I can't deal with this right now."

The truth was that I couldn't deal with it at any time. Because I didn't want it to even be something to deal with.

Riley nodded and sat down on the couch. I cursed myself for not having the foresight to buy another chair for the living room. I sat on the armrest. It was weak, I knew, but if I sat on the floor, I'd feel like an idiot. Besides, having the high ground was better psychologically.

"Shoot," he said.

And for a second, I considered it. That would be one way to end my problems.

"It's the Russians. They created Flying Bicycle Productions and made the movie." I said it so quickly that the words practically spilled out of my mouth. A mouth that, just a few seconds ago, had touched his mouth. I suppressed a shudder.

He frowned. "The Russians? Are you sure?" From his reaction I gathered that he was surprised by this information.

"That's what Zeke said."

Riley nodded. "Then it must be legit. So they stole my book and made it into a movie? Why?"

I threw my hands up. "Maybe they thought it would discredit us. Or maybe they wanted to show that they had access to covert activities?"

"That might be something. They wanted the CIA to know they were up on our cases."

"It seems like a long way to go to prove that. Why not just publish your book and mass-market it?"

Riley flinched. He was still smarting about the missing manuscript.

A question popped into my head. "How did you realize it was missing?"

"I kept it in a safe in my bedroom."

His saying *bedroom* made me weak in the knees. Maybe Kelly was right.

"Well, if they've had it long enough to make the actual film, it's been out of your safe for a while. Maybe even a year."

Riley rubbed his face. "I swear, I had no idea it was gone."

I changed the subject. "Did you find Gruff and Ferret?" From the look on his face, I realized he wasn't familiar with my nicknames for my captors. I explained.

"No. They're laying low."

I shifted uncomfortably. "What was in the script that they wanted so badly?"

A cloud descended over his face. He didn't want to tell me.

"How does the book end, Riley?" I grumbled.

Nothing.

"You know what they were looking for."

He nodded. "I know what they are looking for."

CHAPTER SIXTEEN

"Why didn't you tell Rex? Why didn't you tell me?"

Riley buried his face in his hands.

I got up and gave him a shove. "Answer me! What's in the book that's so bad?"

He shook his head. "I just can't believe they'd include that in the script."

My patience was running out. "What? What did they include?"

"I'm going to end up in prison. Or assigned to Antarctica." He was muttering now, completely ignoring me.

All feelings I might have been feeling were now gone. In their place was a rising fury that I hadn't seen in a while.

"Dammit, Riley! Tell me what the hell is going on, or I'm going to shoot you!"

I was looming over him. Riley's expression cleared…as if he were seeing me for the first time. Which would kind of piss me off because of the kiss and all.

"I was going to edit it out if I ever sold the book." He licked his lips. "I swear I only included it to ramp up the ending."

I considered punching him. The shotgun behind the couch was another option. But I decided to give him one more chance.

"Tell me what it is, and I'll help you."

There. I'd said it. Even though a little while earlier I'd sworn off the whole mess. Now I was back in it.

"Okay." He paused for a moment and got to his feet. "You have to realize that I wrote this, but didn't really think it was ever going to see the light of day. You have to believe that before I tell you."

If I agreed, then I was taking on more responsibility for this case than I wanted. And I was pretty sure that when I heard what it was, I was going to punch Riley hard.

"Fine. I believe you."

"You might want to sit down for this," Riley said.

"I'll stay standing, thank you." I didn't have time for this crap.

"It's the Yaro Plans."

I sat down.

"You," I uttered as I pointed at him just to be clear. "You wrote about the Yaro Plans?"

He nodded. He didn't look too good. For a moment, I thought he was sweating. Riley never sweated.

"Why on earth would you have done that?" To be honest, I was sweating too.

"It just fit into the story so well—the whole plot would've fallen apart without it. I was going to replace it with something else…only I never got around to doing that."

"Who are you?" I asked.

"What?"

"Who are you? The Riley Andrews I know would never ever have mentioned the Yaro Plans."

Once again, he buried his face in his hands. "I never would've guessed that they'd take the book. My safe was booby-trapped for crying out loud. And no one knew where I lived!"

"Obviously someone not only knew where you lived but also knew what you'd been writing and where you'd put it!"

The Yaro Plans! It was hard to even think about, let alone say out loud. This was a document that outlined a new technology that allowed us to enter into other computers anywhere, anytime. A kind of back door built into the software of the two biggest companies—Yaro allowed the CIA to remotely enter into encrypted computers. We could pull data in any format in seconds. The secret was a special satellite we'd launched into space.

There wasn't another country in the world who knew we had the ability to do it. Not even our allies knew. As far as I knew, it hadn't been activated yet, but when I had left they were very, very close.

And the worst part, besides scaring our enemies and infuriating our allies, was the fact that these two software giants had no idea we'd even done it. The programmers who made it happen were actually CIA plants. They'd worked in these companies for years.

Riley's screw-up wouldn't just make the entire world want to destroy us, it would also create major problems between the Agency and US corporations. And since none of this was even legal, lawsuits and investigations would soon follow. It might even be the death knell for the CIA.

"How much detail did you include in the book?"

Not that I completely understood it. I wasn't a computer expert. But I knew it was there and what it meant for my country should that intelligence find its way into the wrong hands…which at this point…would be just about everybody's.

"Does it matter?" Riley groaned.

"Probably not, but I'd like to know." I could barely keep an edge out of my voice.

"I barely mentioned it. Well, I gave it a different name, but described it and what it does. But that's it."

Closing my eyes, I leaned back against the couch. I ran through various possible reactions in my head, exploring every possible outcome. My training kicked in as I assessed the damage and thought about damage control.

"So both the book and the script have the information. Both are missing?"

Riley nodded. "I think so. I never finished reading the script."

The Russians had taken the book and made it into a film. Why? To let the world know about the Yaro Plans. To humiliate and possibly bring down our government. To stir unrest between corporate and national interests.

"The Agency must know about it. Why else would they shut the movie down all across the country the moment it aired for the first time?"

"I think so," Riley said. "Which means someone on the Russian side told the feds about it."

"Thank God they did," I murmured.

I thought about yelling at him again. But I couldn't do it. I'd made some really stupid mistakes in the field too. And no, I'd never talk about them. Ever.

This was huge. But this was something Riley had kept private. He never thought anyone would see it before he could change the manuscript. A flood of empathy washed over me, and I was exhausted. I wasn't mad at Riley anymore, but I was overwhelmed by the fact that this would be nearly impossible to track down. The book and the script could be anywhere. And there could be copies.

"Why did they take the script back?" I asked out loud. "Surely they made copies. So why did they need that one? And why did Tim Pinter have it in his car?"

"There's another possibility." Riley rubbed his chin. "Pinter could've been coming to you to hide it. Maybe he wasn't ex-CIA after all?"

"Why me? Out of the millions of people in the country, why me?"

"Because you are retired. Because you are still loyal." Riley ticked off explanations on his fingers. "And because you live in the middle of nowhere."

"But that's just it! No one should be able to find me! When I left Langley, I left my old life behind. And yet the CIA drops by to mess up my life every other month!"

I'd come back to Who's There, Iowa to hide out. To get away from it all. I'd changed my identity, which was good because my real name was Finnoughla Merrygold Czrygy. Wrath was Mom's maiden name. And that still hadn't stopped people from finding me over the past two years.

"I think it might be worse than we thought," I said slowly. "I think there's a mole in the Agency."

Riley groaned. "That's bad. Really bad."

I agreed with him. "I'm going to blame Abed."

Abed was an employee of the CIA who loved Girl Scout cookies to a point where he didn't think clearly. And he still owed me money. And I didn't particularly like him.

"He doesn't have anywhere close to the right security clearance."

Damn.

"So what do we do now?" I asked.

We sat in silence together on my couch, each puzzling the situation out. From the endless lack of talking, I guessed that we'd both hit a wall.

"So…" I finally broke the silence. "We know why the movie was made and why the script is so important. We think that Gruff and Ferret were Russian spies and that's why the script was taken. We are guessing that Tim Pinter might have stolen the script back and tried to bring it to me for safekeeping.

"What we don't know is who took the book in the first place or where it is now. We don't know for sure that Pinter was on our side, but even if he was, we don't know who killed him or how."

Saying it out loud didn't make things any easier to understand.

"And I have a couple of other questions," I said. "Why haven't the feds interrogated me yet? Who told them about the movie? And do they even know that you had the Yaro Plans out for everyone to see?"

Riley cocked his head to one side. "I hadn't thought of that. It's possible that the Agency doesn't know what was in the book. They might not even know about its existence. And we don't know for sure that the Yaro Plans are mentioned in the movie."

"I think it's safe to say they are," I said. "That's the only thing that could explain the Russian involvement."

"We have to find Gruff and Ferret," Riley said at last.

I nodded. "We have to find Gruff and Ferret."

* * *

We drove around town for an hour, inspecting every road, alley, and driveway, but found nothing. It was time to move to the secondary tier and hit all the barns, storage facilities, and warehouses on the perimeter. I'd suggested we do that first, since I knew the men had kept me in a place like that, but Riley was taking no chances. He'd hoped we'd get lucky and find a little ranch house with the car in the driveway.

But no such luck, so now we were following the perimeter. Every two minutes we'd stop and get out of the car to inspect a huge building. But after half an hour, we'd turned up nothing. Most people might have given up and gone home. But then we weren't most people. We were spies. And spies go through every single possibility until they've all been spent.

"This is not working out," Riley said as we got back into the car.

We'd just searched the last possible place—the school administration's warehouse. It was full of books and chairs. No surprise there. What we didn't find was a large man with a deep voice or a small man with a high-pitched voice.

It was getting late. Rex would be wondering what had happened to me. I dropped Riley back at my house and parked in the garage on the alley.

"Where have you been?" Rex asked the minute I walked in the door.

He looked me over, noticing the dirt and grime that was all over me. Warehouses are very dirty places.

I slumped into the kitchen chair and leaned my head back against the wall.

"Out looking for those guys," I said. There was no way I was telling him about Yaro. That way he wouldn't get pulled into the mess that was bound to come next.

"You're telling me that you went out to find the men who kidnapped you?"

"When you say it that way, it sounds stupid," I muttered.

"That's because it is stupid." Rex didn't raise his voice—he lowered it. That was all he needed to do to show the gravity of the situation. Most people raised their voices as they got angry. Not my boyfriend.

I was too tired to argue. "I know. You're right. It was a stupid thing to do."

But Rex was still angry. He pulled a bottle of beer out of the fridge and went into the living room. I heard the TV turn on. I took that as my opportunity to go upstairs and take a shower.

You might think a gun is a spy's best friend. But it isn't. It's a shower. I'd been in enough hellholes around the world to know that mud, camo face paint, and blood could be washed away under a piping hot shower nozzle.

That doesn't mean it's easy to find one. I'd been in places where a shower consisted of a bucket outside. The CIA rarely put agents up at The Ritz. The word *shower* has a loose meaning in my former world.

But here, in Rex's house, it meant a hot, steamy shower where the hot water never runs out. It meant soft, fluffy towels and shampoo that smelled good. I took my time and enjoyed it. If Riley got busted, I might get busted too. And I wasn't too sure about showers in prison.

I'd just gotten into my bedroom when my cell buzzed. I answered. It was more dangerous not to.

"Where have you been?" Kelly chastised me. "You do know that the mud run is tomorrow!"

Oh right. That. "Of course! Wait, aren't you supposed to be in Omaha?"

"I am in Omaha. Soo Jin said she's been trying to get hold of you. So I called."

Right. Soo Jin. Kelly's new best friend. Maybe that was okay, considering I might be spending the rest of my life at Leavenworth.

"I'm here. I'm just getting ready for bed. Calm down."

"I left my minivan for you, and Soo Jin is renting one. You'll meet at the school at ten in the morning."

"I know. I've got it all." I didn't. Not really. The news about the minivan was a surprise, but I couldn't let Kelly know that.

"Good luck. Do you think Riley could film it? I'd love to see that."

I rolled my eyes, but she didn't need to know that. "I don't see how he can. The course is a couple of miles long, and unless he wants to run beside us, which I don't think he'll want to do, he can't film it."

That wasn't the real reason. The real reason was that I needed a break from Riley, the CIA, mad Russians, and secret plans. The mud run would be perfect. I could clear my head and possibly die from lack of exercise. That was one way of getting out of prison.

"Alright then." She sounded disappointed. "Good luck."

"Don't worry about a thing. We've totally got this."

"No cheating. I mean it."

"I heard you the first time. It'll be fine."

Oh, after the week I'd been having, cheating was totally on the table.

We hung up, and I stretched out on the bed. It would've been nice if Rex stopped by my room to make sure I was okay. He didn't. Neither did my cats. They must have gone to bed with him. Again. The little traitors. That was one reason why moving in together wouldn't be a good idea. I'd never get my cats to myself again.

Most people wouldn't be able to sleep with the possibility of prison hanging over their heads. I didn't have that problem. You took your sleep when you could as a spy. Falling asleep was no problem.

Besides, tomorrow I had bigger fish to fry in the form of Brian Miller and his Boy Scout troop. Soo Jin and I would need all the help we could get.

I hadn't really told Kelly we *wouldn't* cheat…

CHAPTER SEVENTEEN

The camp was packed when we arrived and checked in. As the driver of the first car filled with giggling and screaming little girls, I picked up the packet with our numbers and the safety pins to attach them to our clothes.

To my relief, the girls were tricked out in tactical clothing. Cargo shorts, T-shirts, running shoes, and baseball hats that all said *My Leader Can Beat Up Your Leader.*

I wasn't too sure about these, but Lauren's mom had them made, so I didn't think I should say no. Besides, secretly, I liked them. And I was pretty sure, should it all disintegrate into a melee between leaders, I could take each and every one of them.

We parked the vans and got out. Soo Jin and I helped pin the tags on everyone. She'd brought old-fashioned stick candy to "sugar the girls up." She said that was all the gas station had. Only in a small town did gas stations have stick candy. We looked ready. I pushed all thoughts of prison and espionage aside and threw myself into preparations.

"I'd better go see which heat we're in," I told Soo Jin. She winked. She knew that I already had the heat sheets.

I was really going to scope out the competition. There were three heats with one final winner, based on time, and we were in the last one, alongside Brian Miller's team and two others I didn't know—a high school volleyball team and some group of adults who worked for a nonprofit or something.

Why were my little girls up against all older teams? Oh, we were *so* going to cheat. I just had to figure out how. And I would. We would get to watch two races before ours and see how things worked. It was a small advantage, but I was more than willing to take it.

The volleyball team looked pretty hard-core at second glance. These girls were serious athletes and not afraid of diving to the ground, as was evidenced by the fact that they were running through some drill that required them to dive onto the ground. The group of adults was even more unsettling.

"Who are they again?" I asked Soo Jin, who'd just joined me.

She pulled the schedule out of her pocket and frowned. "A last-minute entry, I guess. Says they're from Coats for Cats, some nonprofit in Des Moines."

Cats needed coats?

I sized up the adults dressed in military boots and camouflage clothing—a few of them had ski masks on. I'd never heard of the nonprofit, but that didn't necessarily mean anything.

"I think I'll say hello," I said.

The only one not doing stretches that looked like they were out of a 1950s calisthenics playbook was a severe-looking woman with very short, black hair and a grimace. I almost thought she was a man until I noticed no Adam's apple.

"Hi!" I said with my bubbliest grin. "I'm Merry. My troop of third-graders is running against your team." I stuck out my hand for good measure.

The woman glared at me, and then my hand, before turning and walking away.

Oh. So that was how it was going to be. Fine.

"How do they look?" Soo Jin asked when I'd returned.

"Like they want to kill us for sport," I answered.

"Don't you think the ski masks are a bit much?" Soo Jin bit her lip.

"Intimidation factor." I couldn't take my eyes off them. "I don't think it will affect our girls."

I looked over and saw Betty shouting as she walked up and down a row of our girls, who were standing at attention. They'd put camo face paint on, and Betty was smacking a riding crop against her hand.

"Is she speaking German?" Dr. Body looked a little horrified.

"I think she's just using an accent." We moved closer to hear what I assumed was supposed to be a pep talk to the troop.

"We are the destroyer of hopes and dreams!" Betty shouted. "The devourer of men's souls!"

"Devourer?" Soo Jin asked.

"I'm impressed she knows that word," I replied.

"They..." Betty aimed her riding crop at the other teams. "...think we're pushovers! They think we're just a bunch of little girls! That is *our* advantage and *their* downfall!"

"Where did she get this speech?" Soo Jin asked.

I was transfixed.

"This is where we fight and they die!"

"Is that from the movie *300*?" Dr. Body whispered.

"When you put your hand in a puddle of goo that used to be your best friend's face..." Betty's face was inflamed.

"That's from *Patton*," I said.

"We few, we happy few, we band of Girl Scouts..." the girl continued.

"Henry V," Dr. Body mused.

Apparently, Betty had googled war speeches the previous night. And the girls loved it.

"Should we stop her?" Soo Jin asked.

"Nah," I said. "She's on a roll. Let's go ask who's in charge. I want to know more about our adversaries."

"Dr. Body!" A young woman ran up to us as if she could read minds. "We're so glad you're here!"

"Is someone hurt?" Soo Jin asked.

The woman looked confused. "Um, no...we're just glad you're here."

Soo Jin introduced me to Allie Maddox.

"Miss Maddox?" I asked. "Who are the adults in ski masks?"

"Allie, please," the woman said as she looked around. "Who? Oh!"

"Yes, them."

Now they all had ski masks on and were stretching and cracking their knuckles.

Allie frowned as she looked at her clipboard. "Well, it says they're from Coats for Cats. But those ski masks..."

I nodded. "Not appropriate."

"It'll intimidate the girls," Soo Jin added. "Isn't this all supposed to be for fun?"

"You should go over there and ask them to tone it down a bit," I suggested.

Allie looked like she'd rather set fire to her own hair and put it out with a cheese grater than approach the group. "Um, okay, I'll talk to them."

We watched as she joined the team from Coats for Cats. The volleyball team was now doing a group chant—something about bathing in the blood of their opponents. And the Boy Scouts, still in uniform, all had Mohawks and blue faces. It was like a bizarre version of *Braveheart*.

Allie approached someone and started talking. Whoever it was refused to remove his ski mask, and a very shaken young woman rejoined us.

"They said it's because a couple of them are disfigured and they're all wearing masks out of solidarity or something." She trembled a little.

"Do you want me to go over there?" I asked. I would. And I'd get them to take off those masks. They didn't scare me.

"N-no." Allie didn't seem convinced. "And they requested the lane next to yours."

I spun around to look at the group. My spy-dey senses were tingling. Something was off here, but what? I couldn't remember pissing off anybody in Des Moines since I'd moved here. Maybe they were mad that I didn't have coats on my cats.

"So I'm putting you in the middle, between the Boy Scout troop and them." Allie gave us a frail smile before darting off on a make-believe emergency.

"This doesn't seem like a good idea," I said.

"Maybe we should drop out." Soo Jin looked nervous. "I don't want the girls to get hurt, and between Brian Miller's troop and these psychos, I think we might be in trouble."

I nodded. "You might be right. Let's talk to the girls."

Our troop had divided itself into two groups and were slapping each other on the bellies like sumo wrestlers preparing for battle. Their little faces wore expressions of utmost seriousness. These kids were not going to like the idea of quitting.

"Ladies!" Soo Jin stepped in their midst, and they stopped slapping and turned to listen. "The other teams in our heat are a lot older than us. I was thinking that we…"

"Change heats?" Inez asked.

Dr. Body looked at me as if to ask why we hadn't thought of that. "That might be a good idea."

The Kaitlyns stepped forward as a group. One of them had a necklace made of doll heads and two others had a necklace of what I assumed were those same dolls' fingers. The fourth Kaitlyn was wearing Barbie shoes on a necklace. Apparently, she'd misunderstood what these girls had decided to do.

"Not a chance," said the one I thought was Brian's sister. "We do this the right way, or we don't do it at all!"

The girls let out what sounded like a Native American war whoop before Caterina pulled out a set of bagpipes and started playing a war song. That was new…

"Maybe we shouldn't do it at all," Dr. Body answered.

The girls fell silent. I was afraid they were going to eat her.

"Freeeeeeeedoooooooom!" the Hannahs cried out.

I shrugged to Dr. Body and decided that when this was over we were going to have a chat with the girls about mixing their war metaphors.

"Fine," I said. "Let's go watch the first heat. During the second, we will come up with a game plan."

The girls nodded and marched two-by-two toward the start of the race, whistling the theme song from *The Bridge on the River Kwai*. As they passed me, I saw that they all had bloody skulls, drawn in crayon, taped to the back of their shirts.

"Well," I said to Soo Jin, "at least they're taking this seriously…"

I was just glad Kelly wasn't with us. She'd blame me for…whatever it was that was happening here.

We stood at the edge of the first obstacle. Four teams, all with kids our age, stood poised and ready to run. The other troops wore their hair in ponytails and had colorful matching T-shirts with nice things like birds and horses on them.

Betty was picking her teeth with a rubber bayonet, which I immediately confiscated, while Emily and Lauren had licked their candy sticks into shivs. The two Hannahs were smacking fists into their palms, and Ava was muttering something about "the lamentations of their parents" under her breath.

Allie stepped forward and explained the course to everyone. Her previous chipper attitude was gone, and she looked a little nervous. Who were the Coats for Cats people? And why cats? Why not children? Sure the winters were brutal here, but did we need a whole organization to clothe the cat population in the middle of Iowa?

Someone blew a whistle, and the four teams were off.

Everyone ran through the first mud pit, some getting stuck and a few moving onward without shoes. They hit the ropes and swung across with ease. That was good. I had been worried about that. All four teams got through the element quickly, and we followed them to the archery range.

At this point, things began to fall apart a bit as the teams struggled to put their snowshoes on. I gave a silent thanks that we had gone snowshoeing the previous winter. That should give us an edge.

The first two girls approached their team's balance beam. One held back to watch the other girl go first. Very carefully, she stepped up onto the beam.

"At least they're low to the ground," Dr. Body whispered.

She was right—there wasn't much of a fall. To my surprise, the first girl made it across with no problems.

My girls were absorbed. They watched as the bulk of the four teams now struggled to make it across a two- or three-inch beam while wearing snowshoes. Several fell and had to go back and do it again. It appeared that the trick was to shuffle sideways across the beam. Trying to walk heel to toe with the added length of the snowshoes was impossible.

I had to admit, it did look like fun. The girls were laughing and teasing each other as they ran to the next element. All four teams lined up at this point. It was slow going. You had to crawl through deep mud, underneath four planks. Touching the boards meant you had to start over. What was our advantage here? The fact that our girls were smaller than the Boy Scouts, the high school volleyball team, and the Coats for Cats people?

Whatever edge we could score was going to be tough. I spotted all three of our opposing teams on the sidelines, watching. In fact, I could've sworn that one of the ski mask guys was staring at me. But ski masks are tricky—like those paintings that look like the eyes are following you everywhere.

That's one thing that, as a spy, I'd never seen. Like in those Scooby Doo movies where someone is really looking at you through holes in the eyes of a portrait. It just doesn't happen in the real world—probably because it's too obvious.

The third element was taking longer than the other two combined. These kids were my troop's age. And creeping on their hands and knees through two feet of muck wasn't working for them.

"I think we need a flamethrower," Lauren said quietly. "You know, to dry the mud?"

I ignored that—mainly because there was no way I could get one on such short notice, and I couldn't see how we could "accidentally" activate a flamethrower and just sit around while it dried the mud. My mind was focused on the next task—the canoes.

The eight aluminum canoes looked like the ones the camp owned. If so, they wouldn't be too much trouble. At that point we'd have to break into two teams of five. I figured that Dr. Body and I could each pull. The smallest girls would go inside the two canoes with two larger girls pushing from behind. Soo Jin and I would shoulder the majority of the weight, and I was fairly sure we could pull it off.

But then again, these other troops had probably thought this out too.

Turned out—not so much. To my complete surprise, the first team to the canoes seemed to not understand how physics worked. I watched incredulously as the adults got into the canoes. As a result, the boats wouldn't budge. Maybe the adults were tired or something, but it seemed to me that they were making a pretty ridiculous mistake.

The other three teams nailed it, fairly sailing over the grass as they did what I wanted to do. The other troop just sat there, unable to move the canoes. Finally, the girls who'd been trying to pull burst into tears and ran off the field. This team was done.

As a group, we followed everybody else to the climbing wall. I was kind of excited about this one. My girls were natural monkeys. I took the opportunity to check out what our opposition was up to.

Brian Miller was standing opposite us, glaring right at us and making a slashing motion across his throat. His reputation had been destroyed by the laser tag game, and he was looking for some payback. The rest of his troop seemed okay, and his goofy dad was making a daisy chain. But I was going to have to watch Brian.

The volleyball players were shouting rude insults at the teams participating. No doubt these were the mean girls at their school. When a little girl on one of the remaining teams started crying, they badgered her with insults. Their coach seemed oblivious. If I had anything to say about it, these bitches were going down. Hard.

The problem with them would be their rabid competitiveness. They would do anything to win and had the physical stamina to make it happen. That team was our biggest competitor in these events. The Boy Scouts were out for blood, but even they wouldn't be able to handle these athletes.

I turned my attention to the ski patrol. It was warm, like it always was in September, and to my immense satisfaction, I watched as they sweat their brains out. A few took off their masks, revealing bright red, sweaty faces. These people were older, maybe in their forties. And most were out of shape.

Three members of the group, however, didn't remove their masks. Allie said something about one or two of them being disfigured. Were they horribly scarred? Because that would be more unsettling than the ski masks were. But I wasn't about to tell them that.

Someone squeezed in between Soo Jin and me, and I found Allie, holding a tablet.

"I'm sorry I can't do anything about your heat. But I can do this. The whole competition is being videotaped live. We have cameras all over the camp. Not many in this crowd will want to follow the contestants down to the lake, but you can."

She tapped an icon, and a checkerboard of screens popped up. Every element was covered in high-definition.

"Thank you," Soo Jin said. "But isn't this cheating?"

Allie shook her head. "Considering what your troop is up against? I'd say this was the only decent thing to do." She slipped away before I could say anything.

"Come on guys," I said softly to the troop. "Let's go strategize."

We found a shady, isolated area beneath a couple of towering oak trees. I explained that we didn't need to continue watching the race because now we could see it live from the tablet. Soo Jin offered to keep an eye out while the rest of us figured out some sort of plan.

"Those high school girls are scary." Inez looked at the others. "I'll bet they're really good."

"What's the lineup?" one of the Kaitlyns asked.

I took a stick and drew four lines in the dirt. "The first team, on the left and outside lane, is the Ski Mask patrol." (I didn't want to say Coats for Cats because the girls would find that adorable, and adorable wouldn't work today.) "We are next, followed by the Boy Scouts with the volleyball players on the other side."

"I think I'd rather be next to the scary high school girls," Caterina muttered.

"This is good!" Emily said. "We can keep an eye on Brian Miller's team. They're the only ones we really have to beat."

An argument broke out between the girls who wanted to win the whole thing and the girls who just wanted to see Brian Miller's troop eat mud. I let them simmer while I gave the matter some thought.

"They're over the wall," Soo Jin announced, not looking up from the tablet, "and heading down to the lake."

Kelly didn't want us to cheat. But she wouldn't want us to go down without a fight either. What kind of strategy would allow us to do both? I thought about our team: me, Soo Jin, Betty, the four Kaitlyns, two Hannahs, Lauren, Inez, Emily, and Caterina. Four of us had to sit out. We all knew that, but who should that be?

On our way there we'd explained this to the girls, and they'd all agreed to it. I was supposed to make the call because the girls didn't want to appear mean to each other. I sized up the group. Soo Jin and I had to race, obviously. Lauren and Betty were the next strongest, and we'd need them for the canoe bit. I was pretty sure the four Kaitlyns were going to insist on participating, especially Brian's sister.

This left the Hannahs, Emily, Inez, and Caterina. Ava was the only girl not here. She was at home with a bad cold.

"Halfway to the lake," Soo Jin announced.

"Mrs. Wrath?" Emily pulled me out of my thoughts. "I think you should take the Hannahs. I have an idea, and I'll need Inez and Caterina."

Could she read minds?

"Are you sure?" I tried not to sound too eager, but this would solve my problem. Girl politics are the worst. I didn't want anyone upset with me.

Emily nodded vigorously. Inez and Caterina grinned. What was going on here? I watched as all three got out their cell phones and walked away.

"Okay. That answers that question."

Now all I needed was a plan and a miracle. And I wasn't sure which one to ask for first.

CHAPTER EIGHTEEN

Before I started figuring out how we were going to do this, I had to know what Emily and the other girls were up to. They just kept giggling. Then again, maybe I didn't want to know.

"At the lake. On the paddleboards. This heat is almost over," Soo Jin said.

We crowded around the tablet. This was something we weren't sure about. Technically the girls were too young to use the paddleboards. Allie had assured Soo Jin that this was okay because there'd been a drought this summer and the lake was only about three feet deep. Also, they had a literal battalion of lifeguards in kayaks waiting to assist.

The three remaining teams were on the beach—each team had four girls on paddleboards (this was because the camp only had sixteen of the boards that looked very similar to surfboards). They held long paddles that they used to propel them across the water. It was really close. Probably because the girls were all the same size.

"Have you done that before?" I asked Soo Jin.

She shook her head. "I used to surf though."

Of course she had.

"How hard could these be?"

I squinted at the screen. "I wonder why they didn't use their adults for this part."

Soo Jin shrugged. "They're probably trying to be fair. They know it's better for the girls to compete against other girls like them."

"They only have kids. Our two other teams are older than our girls," I grumbled. "I think you and I should be on the boards for sure."

"I can do it." Lauren raised her hand. "I've done it before when camping in Wisconsin."

"Good," I said. "We need one more. Has anyone else ever done this before?"

Only one raised her hand. It was the Kaitlyn whose brother was Brian Miller.

"It's only right that she does it," one of the Hannahs said.

Betty agreed. "It's her destiny."

"Great," I said. "You two watch this leg of the course."

Lauren and Kaitlyn crowded around the tablet with Soo Jin. I took the opportunity to draw the rest of the course in the dirt. Isn't that always what they did in the movies? Anyway, it looked cool.

"Done!" Soo Jin announced.

"How did it go?"

"Pretty much like you'd think. The next teams are lined up at the beginning."

"Alright, girls, from my estimation we have about twenty minutes to come up with a brilliant plan of attack. Ready?"

We spent just under twenty minutes going over ideas for the course. It helped that the girls had seen the first heat. Soo Jin continued to monitor the second heat. Was the plan perfect? Not really. But it was totally doable. I could live with totally doable.

"We'd better go take our places," Dr. Body said.

She handed the tablet to Inez, and that was when I remembered that those three were up to something. Not that I minded. If it was something that would help us, I was all for that. But just in case, I pulled them aside.

"What are you going to do?" I asked.

Emily giggled. "Don't worry. It'll be fine."

I looked at the three girls, hoping to read their minds. It didn't work.

"You can't cheat," I said only half-heartedly. "Mrs. Albers said no cheating."

I figured that since I'd reminded them, I was no longer culpable. Maybe I was better off not knowing. Then later I could claim innocence.

The other teams were ready to go when we got there. The volleyball team was huddled together, chanting something about being number one. The Boy Scouts said nothing. It looked like they were trying to focus on their mental game. That didn't bode well.

The ski-masked team just stood there, staring at us. Now I was worried. This team wanted to be next to us. Now we were their main focus.

"Okay!" Allie stepped onto the course in front of us. In the distance I could see the first few teams coming back, covered in dried mud.

"Remember this is just for fun." She made sure to look knowingly at the other three teams. "Let's have a good time out there! It's all about helping Girl Scouts! The teams' entrance fees go to fixing up this camp." She stepped back quickly.

I turned to my team. "Okay, remember the plan. Dr. Body goes first, and I bring up the rear until we get to the canoes. Look to her for cues. We can totally do this. I know we can."

Alright, so it wasn't Henry V. It was more like Wrath 2.0.

"Ready!" the girls cheered.

Out of the corner of my eye, I spotted some movement near the volleyball team. Was I seeing things? It looked like Caterina was walking right up to them.

"Good luck!" Caterina grinned—her two front teeth missing. "I hope I grow up to be as cool as you guys are!"

This hard-core team that I imagined ate kittens went totally gooey as they crowded around the little girl, cooing. It was a good idea—Caterina was adorable. And while this was going on, I saw Emily and Inez sneak to the mud just in front of the team and dump something into it.

I looked away. These girls were so cute that it would be impossible to get mad at them. And if I had no idea what was going on, I had plausible deniability.

"Let's line up!" Allie announced as she put a whistle to her lips.

All four teams walked up to the line and trained their eyes on Allie. My heart started pounding. This wasn't a fun activity. It was war. For a moment my thoughts flipped back to Riley and his problems, but I forced myself to focus.

The whistle shrieked, and Soo Jin and the Kaitlyns darted forward with the rest of the girls hot on their heels. I stayed back, and I was glad I had. The boys were off, about even with Soo Jin. They weren't falling for her gorgeousness anymore. The Ski Masks were struggling their way through the mud. They weren't prepared for this at all.

Then I saw the volleyball players. I noticed them because they were still at the starting line and screaming in horror. In the mud beneath them were dozens of spiders of all sizes. It took all I had not to look for my trio of terror who were, no doubt, behind this.

"Come on!" Soo Jin called, and I remembered I was supposed to be on my way.

The coroner was on the other side of the ropes with three girls already. She didn't have a spot of mud on her. I wondered if she was so light that she just walked over the top of the mud like that elf in *Lord of the Rings*.

Lunging forward, my foot immediately stuck in the mud. I used all my strength to pull it out and ran as fast as I could in an attempt to avoid sinking. It was a struggle, but I finally made it just as my last girl and the last Boy Scout swung across on their ropes.

I jumped for the rope and threw myself across to the other side, pausing only for a second to look back. More than half of the Ski Masks were on the other side. The mud was really weighing them down.

The volleyball players were sitting back behind the line, crying. I wondered how Emily knew they were afraid of spiders. I gave a silent thanks that my girls weren't.

One team was out. Only two more to go. I wondered what was next for our little trio of terrorists.

I caught up with the girls at the snowshoes. The boys were in the lead, and Brian was screaming insults at his sister, who was carefully making her way across the beam. I strapped myself in and waited my turn. Only two of the Ski Masks had their shoes on. The others were lost to the mud. I'd be willing to bet none of them had ever done this before either.

As I stood there, it felt like the back of my neck was on fire. I turned to see two men in the ski mask group staring at me. I toyed with letting them know there was no point being sore losers, but then it was my turn to walk across the beam.

It wasn't as easy as it looked. And by that I mean it never looked easy. The girls were light, so they just passed over the beam with no problem. Soo Jin had probably levitated over it. But I was having a little trouble.

Have you ever walked across a balance beam with snowshoes? I've been chased through some bizarre situations before. One time I got away from two bad guys chasing me on foot by stealing a skateboard and grabbing on to the back of a moving pickup truck in Tashkent, Uzbekistan (and I will never ever tell my troop about that).

However, this was something different. The plastic shoes were slippery on the polished wood. There was no way to gain traction. I planted myself on one end of the beam, facing the boys, and started moving sideways. Letting my girls down was not an option.

Behind me I could hear one of the men on the Ski Mask team swearing. At least I wasn't the only one. I was flailing like a non-swimmer in deep water. It took every ounce of concentration to keep control. The other team must have been in trouble too because I felt an arm swipe my back side.

"Hey!" I shouted without daring to look behind me.

Whoever had bumped me said nothing.

There was no time to do anything about it. I'd almost fallen off the beam several times. Somehow, after what felt like hours, I stepped off on the other side. There was no time to even feel relief. My whole team had already trekked over the hill and were at the canoes.

I took the hill in seconds. This part was at least easy. Well, eas*ier*. I arrived at the canoes just as the boys started dragging theirs. Lauren and Betty were behind the canoes, and the other girls sat inside. I took up my position next to Soo Jin, whose team was also ready, hoisted the tow rope over my shoulder, and started pulling.

"Go!" Inez shouted.

Caterina and Emily were missing, but it was nice to have a cheerleader. We managed to close the gap between us and the boys, and we all finished together. Where were the Ski Masks? I looked around to find they weren't in the race anymore, which was fine with me.

Whatever Emily and the other two were doing was insanely effective. I'd have to come up with a special badge just for them. Would the Council allow me to do that?

Two teams were left, and each had five people already scaling the wall. It wasn't a proper climbing wall with handholds and footholds. It was just slatted boards. Soo Jin was at the top cheering on the Kaitlyns, who were right behind her. Once Dr. Body disappeared, Lauren and Betty jumped on and began climbing. The Hannahs were right behind them.

"You're gonna lose!" I heard Brian jeer at his sister on the wall.

She ignored him and kept climbing. Good girl.

I was bringing up the rear, behind the last Boy Scout. Behind me there were two men in ski masks. I guessed they were still in the race. Where was the rest of the team? I thought about the part coming up—the run through the woods to the lake. The boys were in the lead and would almost certainly best us in a footrace. In addition, there wouldn't be enough watchers along the trail to make sure Brian didn't do something to his sister.

I moved faster, clearing the top and climbing over. By the time I got to the ground, all of the boys and one of the Hannahs were out of sight. Looking back up at the wall, I didn't see the masked men. I guessed they just couldn't handle it.

Sprinting toward the path, I decided my main focus was to make sure the boys didn't mess with my girls. It would be hard to know if Soo Jin was watching out for the girls. I'd like to think she would, but if she was neck and neck with the boys, she'd keep her speed going.

Dammit. I must've been way behind because I couldn't see anyone ahead—even Hannah was gone. Granted, the course was twisty, but I had a bit of catching up to do. That's when I heard shouting ahead and poured on the speed.

I wasn't a great runner. I could sprint well, and that had come in handy many times in the field. This run was at least half a mile. I was proud of the fact that I wasn't seeing any girls. They were holding their own.

The shouting grew stronger, and I pushed myself. It wasn't pretty. I was covered in mud and sweat and had the breath control of a beached walrus with emphysema, but if my kids were in trouble...

I rounded a bend and saw the two Hannahs engaged in some sort of shoving match with boys twice their size.

"Hey!" was all I could think to say as I saw red.

The boys saw me and scattered. One of the Hannahs gave me a thumbs-up sign, and both girls took off after their tormentors. So that was how it was going to be. The boys had chosen this point in the race to try to slow down our team.

I was gaining on the group now, and by that I meant I was looking at the backs of seven kids, three of them mine. My legs and lungs screamed in protest as I pushed on to catch up.

"Mrs. Wrath!" Betty was struggling too. "The boys tried to force us off the trail!"

"I saw that," I said. Well, I panted. "Have they tried anything else?"

The girl nodded. "Yeah, but I knocked one of them into the sticker bushes."

Good girl.

The Hannahs passed us without appearing to be out of breath at all. Betty and I moved aside for them. The lake wasn't far now. I just hoped I'd have the strength to paddle across the lake.

With a burst of energy, Betty broke away and ran ahead, and in a few seconds, I was alone.

A grunting noise came from behind me, and I turned to see the two guys in masks from earlier. One of them had a branch he was holding like a club. The other had a large rock in his right hand.

Uh-oh.

This wasn't part of the race. These guys were after me. I turned off the path and ran straight into the woods. If I was wrong, these two would just run past me.

I wasn't wrong. In fact the rock sailed past my head, nicking my right ear. I didn't stop. At least one of them wasn't armed anymore. I was forced to slow down because, without a trail, I was running over downed trees, roots, and other hazards. After a few seconds, I spotted a completely smooth tree ahead. All the bark had been stripped off. It was less than a foot in diameter. Perfect.

I reached the tree and wrapped both arms around the trunk. Spinning around it, my feet connected with both men. They went down. I grabbed the club and brandished it. Both men held their arms up defensively but didn't move.

"Get out of here," I growled.

They said nothing. I didn't have time for this. The guys didn't try to get up so I took off, racing off toward the trail before he hit the ground.

I don't know why, but I was pretty sure they wouldn't follow me back to the trail, and no one else from their team had shown up. It was possible that they knew they weren't going to win so had tried a desperate act in an attempt to keep my team from winning by taking me out. The rules stated that even though only four people could paddleboard across the lake, all ten members had to be at the beach before they could do so. If the Coat group had managed to knock me out, the boys would have won.

Something buzzed my head, but I wasn't going to let a bee or mosquito slow me down. Finally the lake came into view. I stumbled up to the rest of my team just in time to see the boys stepping onto their boards. At this point my run took its toll. Was I going to be able to paddle more than two feet?

"Come on!" Soo Jin shouted as she ran onto a board, the graceful movement effectively launching it into the lake.

Looking back, she froze for a moment. "You're bleeding!"

I waved her and the girls off. "It's nothing. Go!"

Lauren and one of the Kaitlyns followed suit, and I raced to climb onto my board. I think I should be totally honest here—

I didn't look as good as Soo Jin had. As the board moved into the water, I wobbled. To my great relief, I didn't fall. I almost did, like seventy times in one minute, but once I got my bearings, I started to paddle.

You try moving yourself through the water while standing with an oar about as long as you are. Being an adult on a board is good for one thing—strength to pull yourself along but it's bad in that your height and weight work against you.

Behind us I heard Betty, the rest of the Kaitlyns, and the Hannahs cheering us on. It gave me a rush of energy and motivated me to push harder.

Lauren and Kaitlyn had caught up to the boys and were about to pass them when I noticed Brian Miller's paddle connecting with his sister's board. There was no way I could get there in time to stop him. Soo Jin was level with the girls and tried to move in between them, but Brian wasn't having any of that.

"Brian!" A girl's voice reverberated across the lake.

We all turned to see a cute teenage girl standing onshore. She was a slender brunette with killer legs and a smile you could see from the middle of the lake. Standing next to her was Inez, obviously holding her phone and recording everything.

The poor boy's jaw dropped, and he stopped paddling. Kaitlyn took advantage of her brother's stupor to zoom past him. Soo Jin waited for the two girls to pass her before she dipped her oar back into the water and followed them. She wasn't going to allow that to happen again.

The three other boys called out to Brian, but he was lost to them. He'd managed to close his mouth and smile at the girl. She seemed to approve and started waving furiously at him. Brian responded by vigorously waving back. Caterina and Emily appeared on the other side of Inez.

"Brian!" one of his teammates screamed as I caught up with the boy.

"We're gonna lose, you idiot!" another boy screamed.

The girl on the shore started jumping up and down, waving both arms wildly. Brian jumped too in response. As his feet reconnected with the board, he realized his mistake as he wobbled and fell into the lake.

I passed him before he could get back on his board.

"Your paddle!" one of the boys cried out. "Grab it!"

I didn't look back. I just kept going. Within minutes, all four members of my team stepped onto the shore on the other side of the lake.

"You won!" Allie appeared amidst four smiling judges. She was driving a Gator tractor and motioned for us to get inside.

"We won our heat!" Soo Jin smiled broadly as she stepped into the vehicle.

Allie shook her head. "No, you won the whole event! You had the best time of all the teams!"

Lauren and Kaitlyn nodded confidently—as if they knew this was going to happen all along. Soo Jin and I just grinned like idiots. If you'd have asked me at the start of the day if I was going to win, I'd have said we had a fifty-fifty chance.

It took about five minutes for the Gator to take us back to the start of the race, and another ten for the rest of the team to hike back to us. Most of the teams were there, except for the three we had competed against.

The trophy ceremony was nice and short, and as she accepted the prize, Betty shouted, *"Veni, vidi, vici!"*

Inez, Emily, and Caterina appeared—all three with big grins on their faces. In a way, they'd competed too. I pulled Emily aside.

"Spiders?" I asked.

She produced an empty plastic water bottle. "That was easy. We scooped 'em up in the rafters of the lodge."

I wasn't sure I liked the sound of the girls running around, ten feet above the floor, collecting spiders, but I let it go.

"How did you know it would work?"

"When we checked in, a couple of the volleyball players went nuts over a daddy longlegs. I called my uncle at the high school. He's the gym teacher. Told me the whole team is terrified of spiders."

"And the girl at the lake?"

"Caterina's sister's best friend. Kaitlyn said Brian had the hots for her, but she didn't even know who he was. Caterina called, and she agreed to come down to help."

My girls! I was so proud of them! Sure…it might possibly maybe be considered cheating…but that's just splitting hairs.

"And the Coats for Cats people?"

Emily looked confused.

"The weirdos in the ski masks," I explained. "What did you do to them?"

The girl shrugged. "We didn't do anything to them. They just quit after the wall, so we figured we were okay."

I watched as Emily rejoined the team, who were now singing "Le Marseillaise." It's the French national anthem. If you aren't familiar, the lyrics include blood-soaked fields and cutting the throats of the enemies' sons and women. At least they were singing it in French.

Allie appeared beside me with a strange look on her face. "Is this yours?"

She held out a small, military-grade dagger with a black blade and olive green handle.

I shook my head. "No. Why?"

"Because it was thrown at you by those nonprofit people. We saw it on the video and found it embedded in a tree on the trail."

I touched the now dried blood on my ear. "Where are they?"

She shrugged. "No idea. They just sort of disappeared right after that. I googled Coats for Cats—it doesn't exist."

Of course it didn't. "Can I keep this?" I asked.

"I don't want it." Allie seemed glad to be rid of the dagger and hurried off.

I examined the knife. The handle was pretty big. The bottom of the grip moved. I pulled it off to find a small matchbook tucked inside. It was from Joie de Poulet, a new restaurant in Des Moines. Now that was interesting.

Because this wasn't just a mud run. Unbeknownst to me, it had been a run for my life.

CHAPTER NINETEEN

Rex and Riley didn't look happy when I told them the whole story a couple of hours later.

"You could've been killed!" Rex said.

"Kelly didn't want you to cheat," Riley chastised.

"But I wasn't," I said to Rex. "And we didn't…not really," I replied to Riley.

"Have you seen any of them before?" Rex asked.

I pictured the body shapes of the two masked men in the woods and shook my head. "I didn't get a good look at them. But I don't think so."

"They weren't those guys who kidnapped you?" Riley asked.

Gruff and Ferret? I considered that for a moment. "Why would they try to hurt me? They got what they wanted."

"If it wasn't them, who was it?" Rex rubbed his chin.

This was followed by a long, tense silence. No one knew the answer, and maybe we were all just too tired to speculate.

"I'd better get back." Riley stood and gave me a look I couldn't interpret.

"To DC?" I was a little hopeful.

"No, to the house."

"You mean my house."

"Whatever." He scratched the two cats on the chin and walked out before I could say anything pithy.

I turned to Rex. "I think we should celebrate our win."

Rex laughed. "You really did cheat, sort of. Is that what we're celebrating?"

"I didn't cheat." I held one finger up. "It was Emily, Inez, and Caterina. And technically, they didn't cheat either. There are spiders everywhere at camp. And the girl-on-the-beach thingy happened just as he was about to tip his little sister off her board."

"Fine. Where do you want to go?" Rex asked.

"How about that new place in Des Moines?" I tried to remember what it was called without pulling the matchbook out of my pocket. "Joie de Poulet?"

My boyfriend looked at me sharply. "Since when are you into fine dining—or dining outside of Who's There?"

That was fair. Every now and then, Rex would try to lure me to the big city for dinner. He knew I'd always refuse. I'm just a pizza and burger girl.

"I think we need to get out of town for a little bit."

He wasn't buying it.

"To talk about us," I added.

That caught his attention, and he brightened. "Okay. Run home and get dressed. I'll pick you up in twenty minutes."

I ran out the door and across the street. There wasn't any point in hiding things anymore.

Wearing nothing but a T-shirt and boxer shorts, Elmer hollered at me, "Have you seen my pants?"

I shouted back, "Check your house!"

I toyed with escorting him. This was a neighborhood with a school after all. But the old man simply nodded and shuffled back across the street.

There wasn't much time. I'd showered at Rex's after the mud run, but one doesn't wear jeans to a fancy French restaurant. Riley was on the laptop when I came in. After explaining what I was doing, I ran down the hall, not wanting to wait to hear what he had to say.

It didn't take me long to kick off my shorts and T-shirt and slip into my little black dress and ballet flats. I only owned one dress. Kelly had bought it for me so that I wouldn't dress like I was slumming it for her daughter Finn's baptism.

The dress was very simple. Knit material that was fairly fitted but still very comfy. I liked comfy. I ran a brush through my short, dark blonde curls and raced back out the door. Rex met me on the curb.

It was weird that Riley hadn't said anything. As Rex's car pulled out of the driveway, I thought I saw the curtains in my living room flutter. Was he watching us? I felt a little twinge in my stomach.

On the way to the restaurant, I filled Rex in on the girls' overly enthusiastic pep talks. He laughed, and I did too. I relaxed. Rex thought we were going to a nice dinner to talk about our relationship. He didn't need to know that I was still investigating…right?

The conversation remained neutral all the way to the city. We were both sick of this whole *Spy Diary* investigation, and I was starting to feel like an adult, going out all dressed up. Upon arrival at Joie de Poulet, a valet took our keys, and Rex and I headed inside.

The maître d' was a severe-looking man in a tux. The way he looked down the length of his narrow nose told me that this might be a true French restaurant, in spite of the name. Maybe the name, Joy of Chicken, was ironic.

"Have you been to France?" Rex asked as we followed the man to a quiet booth in the back, not far from the kitchen.

I nodded. "A couple of times. I don't like Paris, but I do love Provence. You?"

"No. Someday I'd like to go," Rex answered. He was smiling. He was happy. Why didn't I try to make him smile more often?

The menus arrived along with a young man with slicked-back hair and a spotless uniform.

Rex ordered the wine, and the waiter left us. My eyes drifted over the place. It was nice. Really nice. Perfect ambience, though a little dark. Why would the men who'd attacked me at camp have a matchbook from this place? And why hide it in the knife?

We talked about what to order, and by the time the waiter returned, we knew what we wanted. As the man uncorked the bottle and poured Rex a sample, I scanned the place once more.

A crash, presumably from the kitchen, got my attention. The waiter apologized before running off to see what had happened.

"Do you think we should check?" I asked, hoping this would give me an excuse to walk around.

Rex shook his head. "I'm not on the police force here. Besides, I'm out to dinner with the woman I'm considering spending the rest of my life with." He reached across the table and took my hand.

I looked into his eyes. He wasn't kidding! Someone wanted to spend the rest of their life with me?

I squeezed his hand and let go. "I feel the same way."

Did I? I hadn't thought about it before. Not really. Had I just told Rex I wanted to take our relationship up a notch?

He leaned back against the leather bench looking relieved. "That's good to know. I was starting to think you'd changed your mind about us."

I shook my head. "No. I'm just…it's just…" My brain struggled to find the right words. "This is all happening so fast."

His right eyebrow arched. I loved it when that happened.

"We've been seeing each other for a year, Merry." He took a drink of wine. A long drink. Was he nervous?

"I think I've known since the minute I met you that you were the one," he said quietly.

His hand went to his inner jacket pocket. And I instinctively reached for my purse. It was just a gut reaction to having a gun drawn on you. When all I found was my wallet, I felt a little silly.

"I have a question for you. I was going to wait…make it all perfect and everything. But your decision for a nice dinner out seemed too perfect to pass up."

I shrugged. "Okay. What's the question?"

That's when I noticed the small black velvet box in front of me. I looked from it to Rex, then back again.

"Open it," Rex said softly.

I did. There, nestled inside, was a diamond ring. A gorgeous, square diamond on a silver band.

Oh!

"Rex?" I was afraid to touch the ring and wondered for a moment if I'd been drugged or was dreaming. Maybe the guys at the mud run *had* killed me.

"Merry." Rex leaned forward. His eyes literally sparkled. "Will you marry me?"

I sat there with my mouth hanging open. It probably wasn't a good look for me.

"I know we were just starting to talk about this," Rex said, "but I've had this ring for six months. I know it seems like I'm jumping the gun, but Philby found it and started carrying the box around the house...leaving it on your pillow, on the kitchen counter, in the bathtub. It was just a matter of time before you found it, and I didn't want to be outdone by a cat that looks like Hitler."

I laughed, tears welling up in my eyes. The man wanted to propose, and Philby was determined that he do just that.

And that's when I knew that I did want to marry Rex. Yes, it was a little soon, but we could have a long engagement, right?

"Yes!" I nodded as I leaned across the table and gave Rex a kiss. "I'll marry you." I slipped the ring on and stared at my hand. A hand I never in a million years thought would have a diamond on it.

The waiter stopped at our table and insisted on giving us a complimentary glass of champagne while I just stared at the ring. I was engaged! To a man! Well, I mean, of course it was a man and not a fish or a snowman or anything. My brain was ricocheting off the inside of my skull.

Rex beamed. In fact, I don't think I'd ever seen this look on his face before. I was more accustomed to his exasperation.

I jumped to my feet with my phone in my hand. "I'll be right back!"

Before he could respond, I ran into the restroom and Skyped Kelly, who was still in Omaha. While the phone rang, I thought about all the clever ways I could tell her about this. I could act like I was just calling to tell her about the race. Or I could act very dramatic and pretend something terrible had happened. I was rehearsing my faces when she answered.

"Merry?" Kelly's face popped up on my screen.

All ideas flew out the window as I shoved the back of my left hand in front of my face and squealed.

Kelly saw the ring and started squealing too. A couple of women came in and, seeing that, turned around and walked back out.

"I can't believe it!" Kelly gushed. "He proposed! I didn't think he'd really do it!"

I shook my head. "Me neither? It caught me totally off guard!"

She squinted at me. "Are you in a bathroom?"

I nodded. "Not just any bathroom—the bathroom at Joie de Poulet!"

"Really? I've been wanting to go there." Kelly held up baby Finn, who looked at me adorably before belching.

"So he really did it. Wow," Kelly said as she handed the baby off to someone—or just dropped her in midair offscreen.

"I can't believe it either! We just came here to talk and…"

"Riley finally asked you," Kelly said. "Good for him."

That drew me up sharply. "No, Rex. Rex proposed. Why would Riley propose?"

Kelly looked like she'd been caught leaking valuable intel, and I had this weird feeling in my gut.

"Rex. Right. Sorry. I meant Rex, but Riley just sort of popped out. So many men in your life with names that start with *R*."

"You're not telling me something," I admonished.

"I have to go! Finn's crying!"

Finn was not crying.

"Hugs to Rex! And congratulations!"

The screen went dark, and I shook my head. Of course Kelly meant Rex. I moved to the sink, where I freshened up and then went back to the table.

"What was that all about?" Rex asked. He looked very confused. "I never thought a proposal would send you running for the restroom."

"Sorry!" I could feel the blush creeping up on my cheeks. "I just had to call Kelly. She'd kill me if she wasn't the first to find out."

Rex smiled. "Okay…"

"I'm just so surprised, Rex." I bent down and kissed him again before taking my seat. "And I love you."

"I'm just relieved you said yes." Rex looked abashed. "I don't know what I'd do if you said no."

"You don't have to worry about that," I said.

To be completely honest, a lot of emotions were ganging up on me at the moment. I was floored by the proposal—a combination of happy and scared. I was confused by Kelly's reaction, but she was all messed up from those mommy hormones. And then I was freaked out thinking about the future—a future I wasn't sure I was ready for.

But I loved Rex. I knew that for sure. And after the wedding, when the girls called me Mrs. Wrath, they'd be half-right. I thought about Rex's last name—Ferguson. And here I was just getting used to Wrath, my alias. I'd be Mrs. Ferguson. Unless I hyphenated…or kept my name.

Rex narrowed his eyes. "You look like you're having doubts."

"Not at all! I was just thinking about whether I wanted to be Merry Ferguson or Merry Wrath-Ferguson or…"

He held up one hand to stop me. "I don't care if *I* take your last name. It's a simple matter, and it'll get sorted out."

"You're right," I agreed. "Now where's dinner because I'm starving!"

Rex laughed. "It should be here any minute."

I looked at the ring again. "Are you sure about this?"

He nodded. "Absolutely. There's not a doubt in my mind."

I couldn't help smiling. "Well, the cats will be happy."

"When we get back, do you want to Skype your parents? Or would you rather run off to the bathroom to do it?"

I thought about how happy Mom and Dad would be. At least I hoped they'd be happy. And that's when it hit me.

"Rex, I've never met your parents. In fact you never talk about them. Don't you think that if we are getting married, I should do that?"

Rex squirmed. "Maybe we can go see them sometime."

"How far away are they?"

"Actually…they live here in Des Moines."

My jaw dropped open. "How did I not know that?" I should've done a background check on Rex. What if his parents were in prison? Or insane? Or both?

"Relax, Merry," Rex said. "They're basically normal. They're just a little…judgy."

Well, that didn't sound good.

Dinner arrived with two flutes of champagne. We toasted to the future before I attacked my *magret de canard* (a fancy way of saying duck breast) with a voracious appetite. Who knew that getting engaged would make one so famished?

The food was excellent—on par with restaurants in France. That was nice. And with the proposal out of the way, we didn't feel the need to argue about our relationship. It was relaxing. Soothing. And I was happy thinking that it would be this way for the rest of our lives.

My cell vibrated, but it didn't seem like the right time, so I shoved it into my purse. I never knew I could be this happy, terrified, and worried all at the same time. Yes, there were some issues we'd have to set straight, but it wasn't like we were getting married tomorrow, right?

Another crash resonated from the kitchen. This time, the waitstaff didn't run to find out what had happened. There must have been some really klutzy chef in there or something. Which was too bad because it was the only thing marring a perfect evening.

As he was finishing his *gigot d'agneau pleurer* (a fancy way of saying lamb), Rex grimaced. He pulled his phone out of his pocket and looked at it.

"Merry, I'm so sorry, but I have to take this. I'll just be a moment."

"Of course. Other women might be upset, but I was a spy, remember?"

Rex kissed my forehead and made his way to the front door. That gave me an opportunity to see what had made my phone go off a moment before. As I drew my cell from my purse, the matchbook fell out. Oh right. That.

I hadn't come here to talk about our relationship. I'd come here to investigate. The thought made me a little queasy, but I shrugged it off. I could still kill two birds with one stone. I glanced at the door. Rex was still gone. The maître d' wasn't at his post. In fact, I didn't see many patrons at all. How long had we been here?

The restaurant was small. Only one room. I'd already been in the bathroom, but I hadn't been in the kitchen. All that crashing from earlier made me suspicious. I could just slip away for a moment. At least to find out why the matchbook was in the knife that had almost killed me. Rex would just think I was Skyping people in the restroom again.

I stood up and walked purposefully toward the kitchen. If I was busted, I could just say I was looking for my waiter or that I'd wanted to offer my compliments to the chef. It was a good cover story. I've used more unbelievable stories.

No one appeared in an attempt to run me off as I pushed through the plush leather door leading into the brightly lit kitchen. There was only one person there, a chef, working on some sort of pastry.

"Hi!" I stepped in and looked around. "I just wanted to give you my compliments…"

Something was wrong. The chef was sweating and looking nervously to his left, to an area I couldn't see. Alright. Time to find out what was going on. I moved closer to the man.

"Honestly, that was the best French dinner I've had outside of Paris!" I joined him on his side of the stainless steel counter.

"Were you trained at the Cordon Bleu?" I asked, turning my head to follow his line of vision.

Gruff and Ferret stood just out of reach, glaring at me. Gruff had a gun trained on the cook. I looked at the chef with fresh eyes, and that's when I saw a small tattoo on his wrist that read *CIA*.

Another spy. The Agency knew about this place and had put an undercover agent here. Part of me wanted to give him hell for the tattoo. I mean, really! Why advertise that you're with the CIA? But there was a gun involved, and it was nice to have a colleague in this with me, so I decided to focus on that.

"Hello, boys." I casually picked up a meat cleaver. "What's up this time?"

The spy beside me didn't say a word.

"Did you enjoy your dinner?" Ferret sneered.

"You knew I was here?" I tossed the meat cleaver in the air, applying a spin and catching it easily.

"We saw you through the window," Gruff said.

"You guys didn't happen to be at a Girl Scout mud run this afternoon, did you?"

The two men looked at each other in confusion before shaking their heads. Well, it was worth a shot.

"So what's going on here, then?" I asked.

"That's what we'd like to know!" Gruff said.

Ferret elbowed him hard in the gut. Apparently the man had just given something away. But what was it?

I produced the matchbook and set it on the counter. All three of the men in the room looked at it quizzically. They seemed surprised. If that was the case, why were they here? Was there another player involved in this? One I didn't know about?

"What do you do," Ferret said with an evil smile, "when you have a gun trained on two CIA agents?"

The man next to me grunted in surprise.

"Shoot them," Gruff answered as he brought the gun up.

I threw the cleaver hard and watched it knock the gun out of his hand, causing a little bloodshed along the way.

"Hey!" Gruff shouted as he grasped his wounded hand.

Ferret was reaching into his pocket for something, so I grabbed a carving knife from the man next to me—who wasn't doing anything, I might add. Maybe he was a rookie? I threw the knife, and it embedded itself in Ferret's shoulder. It wasn't a lethal blow. I still needed some information.

"No!" the chef screamed as I hurdled the counter and threw Gruff to the ground. Tearing off a cord to a mixer, I hog-tied him before checking on Ferret, who was too stunned to move.

"Take it out! Take it out!" he shrieked.

I shook my head. "It's better to leave it in. Taking it out may cause you to bleed to death, and I'm not ready for that yet."

There was a gun in his jacket. I pulled it out and retrieved Gruff's as well.

"You weren't much help," I said to the chef who'd gone fetal on the floor and was sobbing. "Hey! You must really be new. They shouldn't have sent you on this assignment."

"What are you talking about?" the man cried.

"The tattoo. You're CIA."

His eyes bulged with recognition. "No! I'm not a spy! *CIA* stands for *Culinary Institute of America*! I'm a chef!"

Well, that explained a lot.

"These guys came in here and threatened me. Said they were looking for someone named Toad." He struggled to his feet and wiped his face. "You threw my knives! Those were insanely expensive! What's wrong with you?"

Rex walked into the kitchen and looked around from me to the two guns I held, to the meat cleaver embedded in the wall, to the hog-tied Gruff, and to the bleeding Ferret.

He sighed as he pulled out his cell and started to tap. "I can't take you anywhere."

CHAPTER TWENTY

The CIA arrived first, followed by the Des Moines police, who were thanked for their time but told they weren't needed here. The maître d' glowered in the corner while the chef was debriefed. I recognized one of the government officials as the extremely intimidating Deputy Director Lewis. I didn't know his first name. He was so scary that it was possible he didn't have one. He gave me a look that froze me in my place.

After explaining what had happened and showing them my new engagement ring (they didn't seem too excited for me), Rex escorted me to our table and insisted I stay put. He went back into the kitchen to give his statement.

I'd probably never find out why a matchbook from this place was in the knife from the mud run. If Ferret and Gruff knew, they'd talk to these guys, not me. This was classified and out of my hands now. I was retired and not needed anymore.

I called Riley. He answered on the first ring.

I filled him in on what had happened as quickly and quietly as I could. If the deputy director found me talking to Riley, I'd be busted.

"I should come down there," he said at last.

"I don't think that's a good idea. You should stay where you are."

"You shouldn't have to deal with this alone," Riley said.

Lewis came out of the kitchen, walked over, and sat across from me. I stuffed the phone into my purse. He appeared to be in his fifties, tall and fit with snow-white hair and steely gray eyes. Very scary.

"I was just calling my parents to tell them I'm engaged," I lied.

"Give the senator our regards," Director Lewis said. He folded his hands on the table. "I know you've given your statement, but I'm afraid that's not enough."

Great. "What could you possibly need from me? I'm retired, remember? I just walked into the kitchen to compliment the chef and found these guys who'd had a gun on me the other day…"

Lewis held up his hand. "I know who they are. And I know what happened. I also know that your fiancé thinks you had nothing to do with any of this."

That was nice to know. Rex had my back. It was a futile gesture but nice nonetheless.

"What I want to know," Lewis said as he leaned forward, "is where Riley Andrews and Maria Gomez are."

"What?" My shock was real. "Maria is missing? How? What are you doing to find her? Is she okay?"

Lewis studied my face with an efficiency that made me think he could read minds. "We don't know. We do know that after the murder in Detective Ferguson's driveway, she warned you that we were coming. She disappeared shortly after that, and we want to know why."

"And Riley? Why do you want him?"

"The reason we haven't contacted you yet, Ms. Wrath, is that we wanted to see if Andrews or Gomez would come to you. We know Andrews is here somewhere. He's just not at your house at the moment."

"You had me under surveillance?"

Cameras. They must've installed cameras. I had a good eye and could spot things like that. But to be honest, I'd been a little distracted lately.

There were two ways I could go with this. I could lie and say he'd never contacted me. Or I could tell part of the truth and maybe they'd leave me alone. I had a feeling I knew which one would work.

"Okay. He came to see me. And he was staying at my house—not that I can ever get him to leave—but if he's not there, I have no idea where he is."

"I'm going to ask you one question, and I'd like a completely honest answer." Lewis had eyes that hypnotized you...like a snake.

"And that is?"

"What was your role in the movie *Spy Diary*?"

This was harder than the last question. I didn't know what the Agency knew. It could be nothing. Or they could know all about Riley's book and this was a test. My throat hurt as I tried to control my expression.

On the one hand, I'd never asked for this. I'd retired and expected to live out a very boring life in the Midwest. I never wrote one word of that story and didn't even know it had existed. Would they believe me?

On the other hand, did I have it in me to sell Riley out? My stomach twisted. It would be a crappy thing to do to my former handler.

You'd think they'd prepare you for this kind of thing in training.

"I'll need your answer now, please." Lewis frowned and lasers shot out of his eyes. Okay, they didn't really. But it felt like that.

I nodded. "Why not? I didn't know anything about it. I had no idea that someone had written up my entire career and made it into a movie. I was just as shocked as you were—although you probably knew about it earlier than I did."

"Did you know that Andrews had written a book about you?"

I looked up, startled. Not because of the book, but because of Lewis's choice of words—*had written a book about you.* He could've said a book about my career...my assignments...but he hadn't. Words really matter in this business. You have to use them carefully.

"I didn't...until just recently. After the movie came out." I felt like a balloon that had just deflated. With those words I'd condemned Riley to a prison sentence or worse...Greenland.

"And Ms. Gomez?"

"I have no idea where she is, and I'm worried now," I said with feeling. "I'm 100 percent sure she had nothing to do with this."

Lewis looked like he was about to say something, but instead got to his feet.

"What's going to happen to the chef?" I asked.

Lewis gave a half smile. "It turns out that we need a sous chef at Langley. He'll be sent there so that we can keep an eye on him."

"He didn't know anything." I explained about the CIA/CIA mix-up.

"We've known about that for a while. At first it was useful, but every now and then some cook does something stupid like wear a T-shirt with those letters on it or gets a tattoo that makes him a target for rival agents. We've talked to the school about it, but they won't change it." He shrugged. "But the chef in the kitchen will be fine."

That was good to hear, although I'd really liked his cooking.

"Congratulations again on your engagement, Ms. Wrath." Lewis walked away.

Looking at my new ring, I thought about how Lewis had said the book was about me. Not my career…me. And how Kelly was convinced it had been Riley who'd proposed. Did that mean he still had feelings for me? He'd kissed me the other night. Argh! Why did things have to be so complicated?

"You okay?" Rex stood next to me.

I shook it off. "They think Maria has something to do with this."

"So that's why you're so upset." Rex helped me to my feet.

"What did you think it was?" Could he see the fear behind my eyes?

"I thought it was because you came here to investigate and turned up nothing."

Uh-oh. "You knew?"

Rex nodded.

"Does that mean you want the ring back?"

"Not a chance." He kissed me and held out his arm. "Let's go home."

* * *

I didn't sleep. I paced around Rex's living room like a caged hyena, constantly looking across the street to see if any lights had gone on, indicating that Riley was there. I also tried calling Maria like a thousand times.

Rex went to bed. He had an early morning and knew I was worried. He didn't really know why. Would he still want to marry me if he knew I was worried about Riley too? He was probably furious that Riley had put me in this situation.

What a mess. I still didn't know what was going on. I didn't know who had attacked me at the mud run, and I didn't know why the restaurant was involved. I could handle all that, I guessed, except for the part about Maria.

It didn't make sense that she was in the equation. It had to be a mix-up. A trickle of doubt ran through my thoughts. Why had she vanished? A chilling thought popped into my head. Was Maria a double agent?

That would be horrible. Maria was my friend. She'd helped me so much that I could never repay her. The girls loved her. Rex and Riley trusted her. No, that couldn't be it. She must be investigating this on her own.

But why would she do that? Why risk her own career to look into a case that had nothing to do with her? That didn't make any sense.

Lewis had said that Maria was missing. He hadn't accused her of anything. That was something at the very least. I may have screwed over Riley, but I wasn't about to let Maria down. I needed to get hold of her somehow.

Was I being watched? The Agency knew Riley had visited. They even knew he had been staying at my house. Were there cameras everywhere? What I wouldn't give for a moment's peace and a burner phone. But how could I manage it? If my car was bugged, they'd know what I was up to. And they had probably bugged Rex's and my house.

Once this was all over, I was going to have Dad's intelligence committee look into that. I was a civilian. Bugging me seemed over the top.

It was late. Really late. In fact it was early morning. I'd practically worn a hole in the living room floorboards by pacing all night.

I had an idea. In minutes I was dressed in sweats and headed out the door. Let them think I was going on a little jog. Unless they'd bugged my underwear…which seemed unlikely and a little gross…they'd have trouble keeping up.

I took it a little easier this time—running lightly for a minute, walking for three. It was still pretty warm outside. It was silent. Dead silent. Nobody was out, which meant I'd notice a strange car tailing me.

Casual glances told me there were no surveillance cameras on the streets, so that was good. I wove my way around the city in a pattern that would confuse anyone trying to follow me. I strained to hear a snapping twig, heavy breathing, or the sound of a car engine idling. Nothing. I was truly alone.

I stopped in front of a new all-night convenience store, whose existence I'd always found strange. A town like Who's There didn't need all-night anything. Now I was grateful and went inside.

The bored teenager behind the counter barely looked up from her gossip magazine. She chewed her gum loudly, popping it every few seconds. Perfect. I bought a single-use phone and paid in cash.

"Is it alright if I use your restroom?" I asked.

The girl grunted and waved me off. Apparently I was annoying her. Good.

The lavatory was one large room. What was it with me and bathrooms lately? I looked at my ring and firmly shoved those thoughts aside. There was only one mission now, and that was to contact Maria.

I took the phone out of its packaging and turned it on. Tiptoeing to the door, I pressed my ear against it to see if there was anything going on—not that the girl in front would notice. I turned the water on in the sink and called Maria's number. I was taking a chance, but my guess was that if they didn't know where she was, they weren't able to track her private cell.

"Merry," Maria's voice answered.

I didn't wait for her to say more. "Maria? Where are you? They're looking for you! I just got grilled in a French restaurant by Deputy Director Lewis himself."

"I'm close," Maria said.

"How close?" I asked.

The panel next to the sink swung open, and Maria Gomez walked in. She smiled broadly and gave me a hug.

"What the hell?" I asked when I'd pulled back.

"Riley set this up before he came to town. The girl up front is an agent."

I thought of the nondescript teenager. "You're recruiting young these days."

She smiled. "You can't be too careful."

"How much of my town is like this?"

Several months ago Riley had set up a fake knitting store as a safe house. I was starting to wonder how much of Who's There was real anymore. Riley and I would have to have a serious talk once I found him.

"Come on. There's a more comfortable place we can talk."

Maria turned, and I followed her, just getting into the dark hallway before the fake panel snapped shut behind me.

"How are the cats?" Maria asked as we walked toward a light at the end of the hall.

"Fine."

"How'd the mud run go?" She turned into a large comfortable room filled with sofas.

Two guys were sitting on one, laptops open. One smiled at me.

"Hi, Abed." I had no idea who the other man was.

I dragged Maria back to the doorway. "You brought these guys here? How can you trust them?"

My friend laughed. "Abed gets a lifetime of peanut butter sandwich cookies for his silence, and Kurt…don't worry about him."

She pulled me back into the room and shut the door behind me.

"What the hell is going on?" I asked as a large screen descended from the ceiling.

You might think it's weird to put a CIA safe house in a gas station in Iowa. But the truth is, there are stranger places. Like a poodle breeder's home in Kazakhstan or a shop that sells snow blowers in Bogotá, Colombia.

"I'm so sorry," Maria said. She really did look sorry. I relaxed a bit. "I couldn't tell you before because Riley and especially Deputy Director Lewis couldn't know."

I threw my arms up in the air. "Know? About what?"

Maria's eye caught the glitter on my finger, and she started squealing like a schoolgirl.

"Oh my God! He proposed! When? Why didn't you tell me?" She held up my hand and appraised the ring.

"Well, for one, it just happened tonight. And secondly, you were missing."

I sounded angry, but I was secretly pleased she'd noticed. I'd like to think I'd react the same way.

Abed and Kurt ran over and stared at the ring. That was weird.

"I can't believe it! I never thought he'd do it!" Maria elbowed the men out of the way, and they went and sat down, dejected.

"Me neither. Marriage was the furthest thing from my mind when Rex asked me."

Maria looked startled for a moment but recovered smoothly. "Congratulations to you and to Rex."

Did I imagine it, or did she hesitate a split second before saying my new fiancé's name?

I pointed at her. "You thought it was Riley!"

Maria sighed. "Yes. Sorry about that. Just a mix-up. You should stop dating men whose names begin with *R*."

That was a lie. However, there was no time for that. I needed to know what was going on, and I needed to know now.

"Why all the cloak-and-dagger?" I asked.

"Technically, it's way above your pay grade…" Maria said.

"Technically, I'm not a spy anymore."

"Right. Right." Maria picked up a remote, and the screen came alive.

It was a view of the police station downtown. They had bugged the station? The only one there was Kevin who was working his way through a dozen donuts.

"I'm sure you've figured out what's going on," Maria started.

"Yes, of course I did," I lied. "But tell me in your own words."

My friend hesitated. "So you know about Riley writing the book. And you know the Russians stole it and turned it into a movie."

"Old intel." I waved her off. "The Agency shut it down because of classified cases and the mention of the Yaro Plans."

Maria nodded. "That's right. They paid the pizza guy to keep an eye on you because you eat pizza all the time."

"Hey!" I protested. "Not all the time." Was I that predictable?

"And the Russians killed Dewey because they thought he had the script."

"Gruff and Ferret." I nodded. "So the Agency brought Pinter out of retirement to get it back."

Maria froze.

"I'm wrong about that part?"

She nodded. "Pinter wasn't working for the CIA."

"So who hired him?" All this espionage was so confusing. "The Russians?"

She shook her head.

"Was it whoever stole the book from Riley in the first place?"

"Yes."

"Can you tell me who it was so that I can kill them and get on with my life?" I was tired and wanted to go home and stare at my ring some more.

"I can. The person who stole the book, gave it to the Russians, and hired Pinter to steal it back from them…"

All the blood drained from my head, making me dizzy. "It was you."

Maria nodded. "It was me."

CHAPTER TWENTY-ONE

I really wanted to punch her. But I didn't. Partly because she had gone all giddy over my ring. And partly because she was my friend and had what I assumed was the most brilliant explanation ever. And if she didn't, then I'd punch her.

"Why? And after all these years of friendship…" I wondered.

"Which were totally real. We worked together for the CIA. And I was legit. Until a year ago."

"Who do you work for?" I growled, fists at my sides.

"It's not like that." Maria took a millistep back, but I recognized the defensive stance.

"You're a traitor? How is that possible? In what dimension is that possible?"

Maria took a deep breath. "I'm not a traitor. I don't work for any other government."

"So what are you then?"

"I'm a patriot."

Patriot. That was a loaded word. John Adams and George Washington were patriots. But then so were Hitler and Stalin.

"You have five minutes to explain before I take you in."

It was a bold bluff. I wasn't armed with anything more than pocket lint. She and the boys didn't appear to be armed either, but I learned a long time ago not to assume anything.

"It all started last year when I was promoted. My security clearance gave me access to very sensitive intel. That's when I found out about the Yaro Plans."

She seemed to want me to react a certain way, but I was still a mess of emotions. And one of them was that I wished I'd never heard of the Yaro Plans.

"I'm not a traitor. I'm a patriot because what I really am is a whistle-blower."

I stared at her. "You *wanted* to let the world know about the Yaro Plans?"

"I wanted to level the playing field, Merry. Something like this…I don't want to say that it's unfair, because it's so much worse than that."

I thought about Edward Snowden—a man who also thought he was a patriot. A man who now hid in Russia.

"That isn't our decision, Maria," I said evenly.

"It's wrong, Merry. One nation, even if it's mine, shouldn't have all that access to everything. Do you know what might happen? What would stop the leadership of the US from using that intel to kill other operatives, start wars between other nations, blackmail politicians throughout the world, or all of the other horrible possibilities?"

My legs were wobbly, and I went to sit down on one of the couches. Abed offered me some peanut butter sandwich cookies, but I shook my head.

"When we joined the CIA," I said slowly, "we vowed to support and defend our country."

"To me, that means even from itself. Think about it for a minute, Merry. One country has access to the only two major software companies? It's too much power. Power no one should have. The playing field should be level. It won't be once Yaro goes into effect. Why should the US have such power?"

"Why the Russians? You could've given it to the UK or Germany. A country less hostile to us."

Maria sat down next to me. "They're allies. What if they liked the idea? What if they just went along with it? It had to be someone on the opposite side. And it doesn't give them the technology. It just…"

"Levels the playing field," I repeated her words.

We sat in silence for a while. I needed to wrap my head around this. Maria was right. I understood that. I looked up and watched Kevin, covered in powdered sugar, as he struggled to open a bag of chips.

"Why involve me?" I asked weakly. "You kind of turned my life upside down."

"I am sorry about that. I really am. It was an opportunity I had to take. The minute I knew about Riley's book, I had to jump on that."

"How did you know about Riley's book in the first place?"

She hesitated. It was clear that she didn't want to tell me.

"You've ruined his career, Maria. You might as well tell me."

"Riley and I worked together on a case and became friends. One night in Estonia we drank too much, and he told me about the book. And about his feelings for you."

I held up my index finger. "Do not distract me with Riley's feelings. Stay on topic."

She nodded in agreement, "Anyway, I saw this as my opportunity to out Yaro."

"How did you get it away from him?"

"I got him to open his safe and show it to me. He passed out cold, and I closed the safe and slipped away with the book."

I said nothing.

"I never wanted to hurt you or Riley. But this is much, much bigger than all of us."

I thought about Maria. She was the kindest person I knew. If you needed help, she'd show up with ammo and a bazooka. I guess I could see how she'd be horrified by the idea of the Yaro Plans. What I couldn't understand was that she actually went rogue.

"So what happens now?" I asked.

"Abed and Kurt go back to Langley and keep an eye on things for me. I've told them they are not to act on anything—just let me know if the Agency comes close to finding me."

"Finding you?" Of course—she had to leave.

Maria nodded sadly. "Russia's offered me a home, but there's no way I'm going there. You know how I hate cold weather."

"I'm guessing you won't tell me?"

"It's better this way. It's the least I can do to keep you out of whatever happens next."

"So this is good-bye?" My eyes welled up a little.

"It is." She hugged me.

"I suppose you're going to turn down the option of being one of my bridesmaids, then."

Maria laughed. "Send me a video." She got to her feet, and I realized Abed and Kurt were gone.

"And this place?" I asked.

"Will be 'accidentally' burned to the ground in the wee hours of the morning. Faulty wiring, I'm afraid. So dangerous."

We laughed, but I didn't feel better. I was still extremely conflicted as I walked out into the rear parking lot. I looked back and saw a spark go up. It turned into flames a few moments later. I ran to the front to make sure the teen at the counter was gone. She was.

I ran inside and grabbed a pint of Ben & Jerry's and a box of plastic spoons before the front of the building caught fire. Sitting on the curb across the street, I dug in and watched the fire. I ate the whole pint.

It didn't take long for the fire department to arrive, quickly followed by Rex and an ambulance. He didn't see me, and I didn't make my presence known. I wasn't going to lie to Rex about Maria. But I could give her a little more time to get away. I liked her too much to turn her in right now.

I got home before Rex and snuck into my house to see if Riley was there. He wasn't. I called him. He didn't answer, but I left him a message explaining that I needed to see him. Depressed and exhausted, I walked across the street to Rex's house and crawled into bed. And then I screamed.

Philby had left a dead mouse on my pillow. It was actually kind of sweet of her.

CHAPTER TWENTY-TWO

"What I don't understand," I began as I shook the pancake mix. I'd finally started learning to cook. Well, it was just a container you poured water into and shook, but that counts.

"Is how the CIA surveilled me in my own neighborhood." I poured a lumpy spoonful of batter onto the sizzling skillet. "I've looked everywhere and can't find so much as one camera."

After I'd told him everything, Rex had invited Deputy Director Lewis over for breakfast in an attempt to get him to leave me alone. No one wants to be watched forever. I'd made up a story about being drugged with convenience store junk food and finding myself back at Rex's place. I never had heard back from Riley.

Lewis gave me a strange look and texted someone on his cell. "I'm surprised you didn't figure it out, Wrath. We had a man on the inside."

"The inside of my neighborhood?" I burned my thumb and winced. "That's rude."

Rex wasn't having it. "How could you possibly have a plant here? We know everyone."

There was a knock at the kitchen door. Rex's kitchen led to the back deck.

"Come on in," Lewis growled. That seemed a little rude, being that this was Rex's house and all.

Elmer walked in and sat down. He was in a suit. He was wearing pants. And he looked about thirty years younger.

"You?" I pointed the spatula at him. I'd have brained him with the skillet if I wasn't trying hard to make a good impression by cooking.

He nodded. "Sorry about that."

Rex took it better than I did. "You did a good job on your cover. I seriously believed you were a crazy old man. What about Ethel? Is she an agent too?"

"My mother," Elmer smiled. "And no, she's not an agent. She really does live here."

Lewis clapped Elmer on the back. He didn't introduce him by his real name, but that's how it was in this line of work. "He's one of our best undercover agents."

I gave up on my anger. "Well, you were very convincing. But I think you went a bit too far with the pants thing."

The deputy director looked confused. "Pants? There was nothing in the report about pants."

I nodded. "Yeah. He either had none on or they were always falling off."

We all turned and stared at him, but Elmer didn't say a word.

I decided for the sake of my own sanity to move on. "One more question." I flipped the pancakes onto a plate. "What about Pinter's murder? How did the killer get out of the room without me seeing them?"

The two men looked at each other.

"It's classified," Lewis said finally.

I wondered if that meant that the Agency had killed Pinter. But they couldn't admit that. Especially in front of the policeman in the form of my fiancé. And, quite frankly, I didn't want to know.

Rex stood up. "I'd better go check on that thing in the garage." He walked out the door because he didn't want to know what had happened. He probably wasn't sure how to arrest a CIA agent for murder. I wasn't sure myself.

I narrowed my eyes at the men. I was pretty sure Elmer had killed Pinter, but I'd never get confirmation on that. So I settled.

"How did whoever it was get out of my house without being seen?"

I even put my hands on my hips for emphasis. I was going to get to the truth of this, or I'd lie awake in bed for the rest of my life wondering if there was a wormhole or some secret doorway to another dimension in my guest room.

Elmer cleared his throat. "Well, if I knew whatever it was you're talking about, I'd guess that maybe the killer got out of the guest room before you came down that hallway. He or she probably hid out in your coat closet until everyone was gone. At least that's what I'd guess happened. I don't actually know, of course."

That was the best I was going to get. I was pretty mad about the whole thing.

Philby trotted into the kitchen and sat at Elmer's feet.

"Your cat looks like Hitler," he said as he reached down to scratch her between the ears.

Philby began to make a hacking sound that I recognized, but I decided not to warn the two men sitting at Rex's table. After a second or two my cat coughed up a small, round gray thing onto Elmer's shoes.

"Is that what I think it is?" Rex's fake neighbor drew back in horror.

I squinted at the object then turned back to the pancakes to hide my smile. "We have mice."

Philby had just coughed up a mouse skull. And mentally I made a note to give her a whole can of tuna once these guys left.

* * *

A few days later, after the CIA had cleared out of town (and insisted that they'd never been there in the first place), things started to get back to normal. Kelly and Finn were back from Omaha, and Allie (from the mud run) was at our troop meeting to hand over a trophy and the certificate for a free camping trip at the legendary Camp North Star.

The girls mobbed her, and she didn't seem to mind drowning in a sea of third-graders.

"What I don't get," Kelly whispered, "is the matchbook to Joie de Poulet. How did it get into the knife? And why?"

Maria had sent me a text. The Coats for Cats team was actually her and Abed in ski masks. They had left the knife for me to find and had lured Gruff and Ferret to the restaurant as well. The idea had been that I'd arrest or kill the Russians, tying up that loose end. She really didn't want them to get off scot-free. Maria had only involved them to make her point.

"No idea," I lied. It was classified, and Kelly seemed to understand that.

I held out my hand and stared at the ring. It still hadn't hit me. The girls had loved the news, and Kelly had promised to be my matron of honor—whatever that was. The girls were all jockeying for the allegedly prized flower girl spot. I wondered if I could have twelve. Philby could be the ring bearer.

It was all a moot point anyway since we hadn't set a date or anything.

Allie finally got the mob to sit down, utilizing the extremely efficient quiet sign. They sat in a circle around her and watched as she pulled a piece of paper out of her bag.

"I've got a surprise for you." She smiled.

Cries of "*What?*" And "*Why?*" And "*Where?*" went up around her. I thought I heard Betty ask, "*Is it a stack of unmarked and untraceable hundred dollar bills?*" But I couldn't be sure.

"The national zoo is loaning our local zoo one of their animals for a year!"

Cheers went up, even though they had no idea what it would be. I was just about to ask why this was a big deal for us when she revealed the picture on the paper.

"Oh no," I said, but you couldn't hear it over the screams of my troop.

"I don't believe it," Kelly said. "Is that who I think it is?"

I nodded. Mr. Fancy Pants, the king vulture at the Smithsonian, was coming to town.

Was it too late to go back to the CIA?

ABOUT THE AUTHOR

Leslie Langtry is the *USA Today* bestselling author of the *Greatest Hits Mysteries* series, *Sex, Lies, & Family Vacations, The Hanging Tree Tales* as Max Deimos, the *Merry Wrath Mysteries,* and several books she hasn't finished yet, because she's very lazy.

Leslie loves puppies and cake (but she will not share her cake with puppies) and thinks praying mantids make everything better. She lives with her family and assorted animals in the Midwest, where she is currently working on her next book and trying to learn to play the ukulele.

To learn more about Leslie, visit her online at:
http://www.leslielangtry.com

Enjoyed this book? Check out these other reads available in print now from Leslie Langtry:

www.GemmaHallidayPublishing.com

Printed in Great Britain
by Amazon